Iron Hand and Bear

When a geologist who horse wrangler Jake Holley has been
gambling with dies of fever after telling him that he has
found gold, Jake travels to the Telluride Hills to take over his
claim. Here, he does indeed find gold nuggets.

Then a trapper called Lemaitre jumps his claim and leaves
Jake for dead. Badly injured, Jake manages to get back to
civilization where his hand, infected with gangrene, is cut off.
Nearly a year after his 'death', and fitted with an iron hand of
his own design, he goes back to the claim to get revenge
against Lemaitre, where he is attacked by an Indian called
Bear.

It transpires that Bear's betrothed, the beautiful White
Dove, has been kidnapped by Lemaitre and that Bear has mis-
takenly attacked Jake (Iron Hand), believing him to be
Lemaitre. The two men form an alliance and travel together
to track him down and to rescue White Dove. However, it
soon becomes apparent that White Dove has a secret in her
past that will endanger both men and soon both Iron Hand
and Bear realize that they will have to rely on each other's
skills if they are to survive.

Iron Hand and Bear

Alexander Frew

A Black Horse Western

ROBERT HALE

ISBN 978-0-7198-2034-2

The Crowood Press
The Stable Block
Crowood Lane
Ramsbury
Marlborough
Wiltshire SN8 2HR

www.crowood.com

Robert Hale is an imprint
of The Crowood Press

Typeset by
Derek Doyle & Associates, Shaw Heath
Printed and bound in Great Britain by
CPI Group (UK) Ltd, Croydon, CR0 4YY

CHAPTER ONE

Iron Hand halted his mule, Mokie, at the foot of the hill. He took a cigarette paper out of his right hand pocket and laid it across the semblance of a palm on the hand after which he was nicknamed, and then sifted some tobacco on to the paper from a pouch that he also kept in his right pocket. He rolled the paper around the tobacco easily with one hand, licked the edge and finished off making his cigarette before lighting it with a match that came from his left breast pocket, struck alight against the rough metal edge of his left hand. The cigarette was lit so easily that he was puffing a few seconds after making the decision to stop at this spot. He did not even think about how his roll-up had been made, so natural was the task after all this time.

'Well Mokie, guess it's just us two again. This is the spot, I'm darn sure of it or my name isn't Jake Holley.' Mokie twitched his ears and raised his muzzle at this because although he was just as stubborn as most of his breed Iron Hand was one of the few humans to whom he paid any attention, and vice versa. 'Here, boy, I'll get that stuff offa you.' This was a suggestion gratefully received by an animal that was not in the first flush of youth. 'The stuff' Iron Hand referred to consisted of a large food pack and the mining equipment that he used in prospecting for the precious mineral that all men wanted, for which many had lost their lives. For the first time in a while he looked at his metal hand thoughtfully; he had nearly been one of those men and the thought of that day still haunted him. Especially when he considered that his death, unlike that of many others, would have been deliberate rather than some accident of fate brought about by bad planning.

The equipment he had brought with him consisted of a short-handled shovel, a pick which had the head of a hammer on one side and a point on the other, a proper hammer, and a large pan with a mesh across the base that could be used in the search for gold with or without water. He also had a carbine with him and a goodly number of bullets. Not that he expected much trouble on this fairly remote spot, but he had been caught out this way before. Along with his other equipment this would take time to get to the required spot in these hills, but time was the one thing he had. Or he thought he had.

He was here as a prospector all right, yet other reasons for being in the area flashed through his mind.

He was up in the hills of the Southern Rockies in the Telluride district. The area was spectacular if you had an eye for that kind of thing, with wooded hills that led to the blue mountain ranges that made up the Rockies. To a prospector the hills were not just covered in the

6

myriad greens and blues of early summer when every leaf and blade of grass was bursting forth with freshness, they carried the promise of discovery. In his case the discovery had already been made. Up here the air was as crystal clear as the water; a man could feel alive, renewed with every breath he took.

As he trudged up towards his claim with his pack across his broad shoulders Iron Hand could not help remembering Ventman. Gis Ventman was a Hungarian, back in Denver, where Jake Holley had earned a kind of living as a gambler and part-time horse trader, and they had often played cards together in one of the local saloons.

Ventman had come here to seek his fortune, not in Denver where the gold had been played out a long time before, but up in the mountains where he was certain new finds could be made fairly easily. But on his arrival he had picked up the spores of tuberculosis, a disease that ate away his lungs leaving him unable to do much but live on the money of his family – who were wealthy émigrés in another part of the country – and sit playing cards while he waited for the inevitable end. He was only in his thirties but he did not see the point in trying to go back to his family because he knew that the journey back to the East would probably finish him off.

One day, when they were playing cards, he was beaten four times at ponte by the man he had got to know gradually as a solid player who he would meet about once a day in the Apollo saloon in Denver. They would play there for at least an hour at a time. Ventman was a tall, dark man with a cadaverous look. Holley had never said so to anyone, but he reckoned that when the time came, the only reason they would know Ventman was deceased would be because he had stopped talking; just from his looks he had passed on a while before.

'My allowance is not through yet,' he said to Holley on being beaten for the fourth time, 'but I can give you something more valuable than anything you can earn from playing cards.' Holley was interested because although he made a reasonable living from his activities, he was neither comfortable enough from his winnings, nor good enough at playing to rest on his laurels.

'Go ahead,' he invited.

'I was not always this pathetic figure you see before you. I studied the science of geology when I was young. My qualifications from New York State University are impeccable, I have been to other countries, and I have been on expeditions where I have helped dig the fossilized remnants of giant lizards out of the ground, my knowledge of rocks being the key as to where to look for such things. Some of my work is on display in the Museum of Antiquities. I have studied the Earth and what makes up her many facets.'

'Yet you're still sitting here owing a good sum of money to an ignorant son of the soil,' pointed out Holley.

'Well here's a tip for you.' Ventman paused and coughed. When he coughed his face became several shades darker and he often looked as if he was going to faint to the ground. At least he had the grace to cover his mouth, although his contention was that he was no longer infectious. 'Sorry about that. These damn

8

lungs're so full of fluid I'm swimming inside my own body. Where were we?'

'You were telling me the way to get some value out of the ground,' said Holley.

'That's right. The fact is, the Earth is a living thing, only most of the time she doesn't move so quickly. These ignorant fools who hunt for gold don't know what to look for, but I do. You've been good to me, my friend, when others would not pass the time of day with me. I will give you my knowledge.'

'Hey, I only gamble with you to get some of your allowance.'

'You say that, but there are other sources of profit.' Ventman was right. In some strange way his companion enjoyed the company of the other man. It was something to do with his strangeness and the depth of knowledge that Holley knew was in there. It was knowledge from which he had never sought to profit, but it was a facet of the man that he enjoyed.

'Volcanoes,' said Ventman in an almost reverent tone, 'volcanoes, that is the clue.'

'What do you mean?'

'Do you know how gold is made, my friend? I'll tell you. The pressures of the Earth are immense. We who live on the surface do now know how intense it is in the crushing mantle of the Earth. Carbon – common coal – turns into diamonds under such pressure. Common metals transform into gold, and are trapped deep underground.'

'I guess that's why gold is so rare. They just can't get at it most of the time.'

9

'In Colorado gold is rare, but less rare than elsewhere because millions of years ago this land went through upheavals of biblical proportions. Volcanoes spewed forth that which had been lying in the interior of the Earth and the crashing mantles created the Rockies. That is why gold is rare here, but far more common than elsewhere.' Holley found that his interest was growing.

'So what are you saying?'

'Simply this – if you want to find nuggets of your precious mineral you must look for places where the volcano spewed forth such metals from deep in the Earth – and I know a place—' here he stopped and coughed into his handkerchief. 'Curse this ill health! I know a place where you will find gold near the surface, a claim in the Telluride Mountains.'

'But why would you tell me? I might just take the gold – if it's there – and never come back to you.'

'You might, but gold means very little to me now. Listen.' Ventman went on to describe the conditions in a great deal of detail. Holley listened sympathetically, but there was no thought in his mind of leaving the comfort of the saloon to traipse about a dangerous mountain, he was just being a good guy.

Three days later, Ventman was dead.

He got the message from Robbie, the ten-year-old son of Ventman's landlady Mrs Fischer.

He was not particularly surprised at the news, but felt a little sad just the same because the Hungarian had been an entertaining companion. What did surprise him though, was when he was asked to go back with the boy and visit Mrs Fischer, who handed him a large dark-brown leather satchel like a schoolbag but with extra pockets.

'He wanted you to have this,' she said. 'He has some mining equipment too, but you can collect that when you want.' This was a surprise, and after the funeral (he was the only one in attendance except for the landlady, minister and gravedigger) he put the matter from his mind for a few weeks. Then one evening when the cards had been running badly and he had nothing better to do, he ventured to look inside the bag and found a sheaf of papers and some detailed drawings that further outlined Ventman's theories. He was not a scholarly man, but the plans were mainly practical details of how to set up an expedition to get gold out of volcanic rock. The main thing that interested him was that such rock was porous because as it came out of the ground and cooled in the air it took in oxygen. This meant it was easy to mine.

Holley took a good hard look at his life. He was just in his thirties and all he had managed to achieve was an existence on the edge of nothing. He had been married, but his wife had left him for a gunslinger called Texas Sam two years before. He did not have any children and his card games and horses barely made him a living. He had some money put away, but that wouldn't last long.

This, however, looked like an opportunity. He was surprised to find that he had considered the dead man to be his friend. This search for the precious mineral would soon show if his friend's theories were true or not.

11

In this way he had set out on his first expedition.

It had not been as easy as he had thought. He had assumed that not many people would go up into the mountains and risk the dangers there, but when he went to make his claim with the Colorado Claims Company he soon found that not only was the area on the map – Telluride – being well worked over, there was even a fairly substantial town called Columbia. Still he had the means and the opportunity. For the first time in years he felt a stirring of the spirit that had been in him when he was a young cowboy. He traded in many of his assets, and then got himself a hardy mule that could carry most of what he needed – he could get the rest when he got into town – and made his way to the mountains. It was not an easy thing to do, and he almost gave up several times, but he finally came to the place he was seeking.

Columbia turned out to be more substantial than he had expected. There was another town with the same name in a different state and many wanted to call their town Telluride after the area. No doubt they would get their way at some point. The town was situated on the San Miguel River in the county of the same name situated below the San Juan Mountains. The name Telluride came from the kind of minerals that were abundant in the mountains known as telluride ores, and this was the name people used when they were referring to the hills. The town had originally been part of the gold and silver mining boom that started in the 1850s, and was situated in a box canyon, surrounded by steep, rocky inclines and heavily forested slopes. For some reason he felt at home immediately.

Almost at once he found that he was at a superb advantage. Almost none of the miners who had come to this area were knowledgeable about how to hunt for gold. In addition to this, many of them were disinclined to climb to the level needed to find the kind of volcanic deposits in which they would discover the gold. He soon found out there was a reason for this. It was difficult to get up the slopes using horses so a lot of the labour had to be carried out by men going on foot. Since they also had to carry food and mining equipment this meant that because they were digging at random, many would just stay near the town.

It was in that very town, which by this year of our Lord 1878 had become fairly substantial, that he met the man who would be his nemesis. They were linked by a love of cards, which they played in the local saloon. His opponent had quietly assessed the new arrival, and the sure way in which he went about things. Inside knowledge is hard to conceal, and the Frenchman, Lemaitre, a hunter and tracker by nature and trade, was able to see such things in other men.

Now, as he climbed back up the slope, aided often by his artificial attachment, Iron Hand could understand why those who were blind to the knowledge that would have aided their quest, stayed further down. For a moment, so long had it been since his last trip, he thought that he was lost. Then his experienced eye picked up on the faint trail that he – and others – had left behind on the side of the hill.

Grimly he tried not to think of Lemaitre, putting the

thought to the back of his mind. He had other things to think about with the effort of getting up here. Then it was all over and he was at the volcanic basin that Ventman had described so graphically in his notes. It was a large depression about thirty feet wide in the side of the mountain where the soil had fallen away through erosion. Although it was covered in greenery, mostly lichens and grasses, the grey rocks poked through here and there until he came to the site of his old workings. He felt a thrill of joy as he looked at the place that had meant so much to him. It was here that he had spent several weeks of his life digging into the volcanic deposit that he found there and uncovered the nuggets of pure gold embedded in the magma that had carried them from the bowels of the Earth. At the time, just for the thrill of discovery, he had taken some of the nuggets of metal and carried them sewn into a pouch in his buckskin jacket.

Now he came towards the mine workings that he had created through his own labour. The workings formed a distinct entrance into the ground, propped up with the pine wood that was so abundant in the area. He had dug down until he could dig no more. His heart was filled with hope on seeing the entrance, but the cold logic inside his mind told him that he would find nothing there but bare rock and the traces left of the long hours that he had worked there. If nothing else, he could stay there for a few hours brooding, planning what he was going to do with regard to a treacherous Frenchman.

He was mere feet from the entrance when he was alerted by a noise that came from inside the cave he had created so many months before. This was enough for him to pull back, and it was lucky that he did so because he was startled by the apparition that appeared before his eyes. Instead of a lithe Frenchman, much his own build, he was met by the sight of a huge red Indian who was so big and wide that he looked far too large to be coming out of the hole in the side of the hill. The Indian was clothed in animal skins from head to foot instead of being semi-naked like most of his brethren, the skins having been skilfully sewn together into the semblance of jacket and trousers. On his feet he wore stout wooden sandals with thick leather bands attached and these protected his feet. His face was decorated with daubs of blue and red paint like many of his compatriots and he wore a cloth headband to keep his thick black hair from getting in the way of his fierce features.

A lot more worrying for a white man high up on a hillside was the sight of what the huge Indian had in his right hand. It was a war club with a thick stone axe bound to the end. Moreover, when the savage saw Iron Hand he gave a warlike whoop and leapt at him, swinging his weapon of war with obvious skill.

Iron Hand was about to die!

CHAPTER TWO

It was unlikely that if the other man had been able to charge at him from a standing position, that Iron Hand would have been able to create any kind of defence against his attacker. But luckily the Indian was emerging from minor mine workings and was not totally out of the man-made hole in the ground before he began to carry out his attack. This meant that as he began to leap forward his feet were still lower than the general elevation of the area, which made him stumble as he tried to move so that he had to sway like a tree in the wind in order to keep his balance. It also meant that for a short while his attention was distracted from his target. In only a few seconds, though, he recovered and began to move forward again with obvious contempt. Iron Hand could hear the sound of his deep breathing and see every line on his face. It was obvious that the Indian was at least in his late twenties, with furrows lining either side of his hawk-like nose.

Iron Hand had set his pack down as soon as he had arrived at the place where he could survey the site of his former labours. He had left the pack – with his carbine strapped to the top – some distance away when he had gone forward to inspect the site but this meant that he was now far enough away from his weapon to cause him some serious problems when it came to fighting the enraged native. He knew that if he turned his back on the angry man he would risk having his head caved in by the formidable weapon now being held by his new opponent.

His mouth thinned into a grim line. In the months that had followed his first defeat he had vowed that he would never let anyone creep up on him again. Once had been enough, and with the return of his strength he had taught himself to be observant and take note of little details that another person might find insignificant. In this case the employment of such a detail might save his life.

The former caldera was surrounded by trees. Iron Hand knew he could not get to his carbine immediately, but he could certainly try to confuse his enemy enough to try and get access to the weapon. But first he tried an obvious tactic.

He shouted at the man.

'What do you want with me? I'm not your enemy.' It was a useless attempt at placating this unexpected foe, the Indian resumed his charge, his face still flushed with anger, as if he hadn't heard a word said by the other man.

Iron Hand dodged to his right even though his pack was on the bare slope over to the left. He acted this way because there was a group of pine trees over there

17

growing on the rich soil of a depression in the steep slope. He was soon amid the trees which meant that he was concealed temporarily from the sight of his opponent.

At that moment he considered turning and going down the mountainous slope as rapidly as he could to get away from this stranger who was so intent on murder. But the same reasoning applied; if he turned and began to run downwards he could lose his footing and fall rapidly. Even if by some miracle he managed to get away from that murderous weapon, it would take an even greater miracle to avoid being injured by the many obstacles including fallen trees and rocky outcrops that were almost certain to bring such a headlong descent to a disastrous end. It was only when the Indian appeared between the trees that Iron Hand made his move, dodging to one side as the weapon descended towards him. It was so heavy and wielded with such force that it made a whistling sound as it came through the air and embedded in the ground where he had been standing a few seconds before.

He found that his heart was thudding inside his chest and he was taking in great gulping breaths of air as he dodged to the side, around the trees, and back to the clear area beside his former workings that had turned out to be the source of a deadly attack. Although he was not in the first flush of youth, Iron Hand found that he was able to summon enough speed to cover the ground at a pace he had not achieved since his teens. His muscles, already tired from the climb, would repay him at a later date for this further exertion – if he managed to live. The trees were now to one side of him and he heard a wordless roar as the enemy freed his weapon.

'I don't know you,' yelled Iron Hand as he ran towards his pack, but it was obvious that the red mist of anger that had descended over the man had not yet departed. The huge native emerged from the trees snarling, showing twin rows of yellow teeth with one or two gaps in them, the blackness of which somehow made his snarl even more terrifying.

Iron Hand scrabbled at his pack. The carbine had been lashed firmly into place with leather straps in case it fell out; now he was cursing the fact that he had secured it so well. Finally it was freed just as he heard the pounding feet of his enemy behind him. He turned and pushed the barrel of the gun forward with his artificial hand while tightening his good finger on the trigger as he swung round.

The Indian halted yards away with the anger quickly fading from his face. He was not looking at the weapon, but at his opponent's iron hand.

'Move an inch and I'll blow your head off,' said Iron Hand. He was still trembling with anger and fear as they stood there at an impasse holding their respective weapons.

CHAPTER THREE

'Go ahead,' said the Indian, 'white man, kill He-Who-Hunts-Bear, do it now.' He completed this astonishing statement by throwing down his weapon which clattered harmlessly to the ground at his feet. To say that Iron Hand was astonished would be an understatement. The one who had been the enemy just seconds before had turned into not only the subject of abject surrender, but one who wanted to have his life ended at the hands of his former prey! The would-be miner began to suspect that there might be something desperately wrong here, and he was curious to find answers despite all that had happened to him in the last few minutes.

'Say, I can't kill a man in cold blood,' he said, ''spite what you tried to do to me. I need you to tell me what's going on, and then perhaps I'll let you go. Why in the name of Creation did you try to kill me, whatever you just called yourself?'

'I am He-Who-Hunts-Bear in your language,' said the Indian with unconscious pride despite the despair that Iron Hand saw in him.

'I am Jake Holley, nicknamed Iron Hand by those who know me.' Not many of them wanted to know him any more, he thought bitterly, now that his money had run out, but he said nothing aloud. 'I'll call you Bear, just now,' he added. The Indian gave him a mournful look.

'At one time, white man, using name like that would have been reason for death at my hand, but not now, no more than I deserve.'

'You speak pretty good English for a native.'

'That is because taught by one of missionaries. He was great man. Father David. He dead now at the hand of another. I speak a little French and Spanish too for they also had their missionaries.' Iron Hand realized that he was talking to an intelligent man who was capable of learning great things. This made it even stranger that he had tried to kill a white man. His bearing and intelligence marked him out as someone who had great rank amongst his own people.

'I don't want to seem as if I'm bringing you down a patch or two, mister, but why would you want to kill a poor miner like me?'

The Indian called Bear said nothing for a moment as if he could not trust his own words. 'I come here for reason. That reason the papers he had with him showing the claim.'

'Papers? This claim?' The Indian ignored him and still spoke in the same mournful voice as one who knows that he has done a great deal of wrong.

'I look for that which he leave here, perhaps the stuff you white people so worship, the shiny gold, and with

21

thought that it might be his hiding place. Then when I come out you stand there in black hat pulled down low, with same kind of trapper clothes and I feel my blood boil over. I not stop to think but try to kill you. Stupid, stupid thing to do, but one of reasons why I am here.'

'What do you mean? You're not telling it straight, fella, and my hand is getting tired of holding this darn weapon.'

'Son of Great Bear not harm you now, you can put down weapon.'

'Listen, frightened white man be the best judge of what he's going to do,' said Iron Hand. 'Spill your guts, friend.' With every second that passed he was growing surer that the Indian was not going to attack, but just the same he held up his weapon even though his left arm, which had been weakened by his long illness, was starting to ache.

'The one you call Lemaitre, he come to live with my tribe over the winter.' This was not such an unexpected statement. Trappers, missionaries and other white men were often allowed to consort with the tribes for the advantages that they could confer, especially if like Claude Lemaitre they might be able to gain access to weapons.

'Wait, friend, who are your tribe?'

'We are what the white man call Jicarrila Apache, for our women make fine baskets from the straw. We hunt on the plains of Colorado and we plough and grow crops on land beside the river down there, the one we call the great silver snake, you call San Miguel River. We fish in river, like bear, good food for all.'

'I don't understand, why would this Lemaitre have anything to do with you?'

'He promise us much in way of help, in return we show him how to get more of the shiny metal white man love so much. We have reservation far below this mountain on poor land. With weapons we get our sacred grove back and chase off white man or so they say.' Iron Hand looked at him with interest.

'You don't believe that, eh?'

'No, Eyes-of-Grey-Wolf goes to Great Bear and say these things but it is not the truth. The white man is too powerful, such things as giving gold to Lemaitre and getting guns only make things worse. White man is too powerful in the end. Much better to have treaty and get land deal that help us.'

'But you have told me you are a son of the chief; can't you get him to do as you ask?'

'Not after what happened.'

'I don't know what you mean, tell me, friend.'

'There is woman with our tribe called White Dove. She is finest woman who ever lived.' When he said those words about the woman his face took on a softer aspect that Iron Hand would never have thought could be shown by someone with such fierce features.

'You say a woman, what age is she?'

'She is eighteen summers.'

'You want an eighteen-year-old girl?'

'In my tribe we do what you call marriage at age of thirteen. If she had taken my hand I would have married her then but she would not.'

'Why?'

'She said that she wanted to know more about world before she settle down, yet one night when moon big, not so long ago she said she was ready for me.'

'Well that sounds like a good thing.'

'Would have been if not for Lemaitre, he came between us; curse him in the name of the Great Bear!'

'Wait, what exactly did he do?'

'From moment he met her he thought she was beautiful. He was taken by her like many of your men are by our women.' This was true, many settlers had fallen for the native women, and oddly, despite warnings from so-called 'experts' this had often resulted in happy and long-lasting relationships. In fact many of the men who entered into these relationships often ended up siding with the tribe concerned when it came to the resettlement of these people into different land areas according to the needs of the government and settlers.

'So it was he who married her instead of you?'

'I think he went to my father, Great Bear and asked for her hand, but Father he say it doesn't work like that with our women, that they make choice.'

'And she accepted him?'

'No, not like that at all. I think he talked to her of many things, of places that he go to that he want her to see, she liked that, but in the end she wanted to stay, be with her own people. Would travel with me when the time came.'

'Then I don't understand what happened.'

'He go back to Great Bear and ask him to sell White Dove and my father refuse, saying that she is great help to tribe and that only one who could think of selling her

24

would be me. Then he tell me in private never to sell her. She his treasure.'

'So Lemaitre came to you?'

'He come and ask me if White Dove for sale.'

'What did you say?'

'Tell what you think?' The face of the big man was now darkened again with anger, not the blind rage that had seized him so terribly just minutes before, but instead a deep and growing rage at the events of his recent past.

'Wait a minute, Bear! You're askin' me to believe that a woman could choose her husband but you could sell her off if you wanted to the highest bidder?'

'It happens,' the Indian shrugged. 'But not one like her.' Iron Hand shook his head to try and clear it at this. Like many of his kind he was unable to fathom the processes of the native mind, realizing at the same time that it was probably a pointless exercise to even try.

'Tell me what happened then, I presume he kidnapped your girl?' He drew back as the Indian towered his once slumped shoulders upward and seemed to expand with pure rage.

'Yes he did,' but worse was to follow. In direct words, Bear told the former prospector how, when the springtime had come and the snows were melting off the lower ground of the valley they had been given for their reservation, a place that was not exactly made for their cultural pursuits, he had woken one day to find that the Frenchman had disappeared along with what the white man would have called his fiancée.

'But I don't understand how he would have been able

25

to do that,' said Iron Hand. Bear explained that Lemaitre and White Dove had one thing in common; they had both kept their encampments apart from the village in general. She had so valued her privacy that her tepee was actually out of sight behind a bluff of rock, and it was there as the princess she was that she would receive visitors. Lemaitre had camped even further away, at the head of the valley. His presence and behaviour had been tolerated because he had demonstrated to the tribe that he had ample amounts of the precious metal. It was Iron Hand's turn to become angry at that.

'He was showing you my gold that I worked so hard to tear from the ground. I would have killed the bastard!'

This kidnapping alone would have been bad enough, but at least the tribe would have sanctioned the chasing of White Dove and the traitor, with Bear at the head of the hunting party, but just a day or so before this disappearance, Lemaitre had gone to Eyes-of-Grey-Wolf and told him his fellow tribesman, Bear, was wanting to sell the girl after all, that he would take the shiny metal if it was offered.

'But why would they believe a story like that? Surely your own tribe knew you?'

Bear explained bitterly that many of his own tribe were suspicious of him because of his open ways towards the white man, because he had learned to read and write the language of the enemy and had shown them much tolerance and understanding, more than they had ever displayed towards his tribe. When Eyes-of-Grey-Wolf went to the elders and told them the story they

26

instantly ordered his arrest and went to his tepee, which as the son of the chief he inhabited alone. There, under some antelope skins they found a pack with the papers for the very claim at which the two were now standing, and worse still, four nuggets of gold, an amount that could fetch large amounts of money from the white man.

'They did not send out search party for White Dove,' he said in a low whisper, 'said that she bought legally.' He protested his innocence of course, but the hand of every man was set against him, including that of his father. But the chief instigator was Eyes-of-Grey-Wolf who said that it had all been a plot for Bear to gain money so he could go and live like the white man he so admired.

Bear did not take kindly to this and he attacked his old enemy, for it was a fact that they had hated each other since the time when they were children and they had argued over a dead antelope. Others had sided with Eyes-of-Grey-Wolf then, and now they were doing so again. Bear could not help the great hatred that swept over him at this point and he would have succeeded in driving a dagger deep into the heart of his second enemy if it had not been for the other tribesmen who had dragged him off and restrained him. In trying to silence his enemy it looked as if he was trying to prevent him from telling some great truth when in reality he was reacting to being lied about again.

Even his own father, who had believed in moderation, had taken the side of his false advisor at this point. Great Bear sat and deliberated for a long while then he said that his son should take the goods of the white man, and the shiny metal that he so desired and he should now leave the tribe; he was banished unless he could make some kind of reparation or prove that he had not done anything wrong.

'That was when I went away from my tribe in great shame and live on the land for a while. My tribe means all to me, I thought of killing myself in the river or throwing myself from the nearest mountain, but such ways are not the ways of my people.' Iron Hand knew this from other tales he had been told about the tribes. For an Apache to kill himself would have been to take a coward's way out, and these men all considered themselves to be warriors, such a way of ending their lives would be tantamount to a sentence of exclusion from the happy hunting grounds that all men find after their death.

'So I take the papers and read them, knowing that the Frenchman would have got his gold somewhere in these mountains and that is when I trace this claim. I come up here for reason, to see if he gets more gold – can you understand, white man?'

'Well it's a reasonable thing to think,' said Iron Hand. 'I guess if there had been any more gold up here he would have come to this place to look for it.'

'Not just a thought in my head. Tracks were here, you do not see them, but he has been here.'

'How could you possibly know that?'

'Look, traces of campfire and ashes not blown away by the wind and rain,' pointed out Bear. 'This piece of material I find.' He held up a square of cloth that had evidently been torn off some kind of blanket.

'They must have sheltered up here at some point, but it doesn't make sense, unless, like you say he thought there was the possibility of more gold to fund his intended marriage to this White Dove.'

'Marry, who say he marry her?' The rising colour of the big man made Iron Hand regret that he had raised the issue.

'Well, let's say that he was short of funds and needed a way of financing his trip. Gold can be used anywhere, even in its raw form. Maybe he thought there would be more.'

'You did too, white man.'

'This equipment I have here with me?' Iron Hand shook his head. 'I don't know what I was thinking. Guess I considered coming back here to see what remained, sort of like surveying the scene of a disaster in which you were involved. You know there's no point, and then you move on.' He looked at his iron hand. 'I guess I need to move on a lot more than I thought.' He did not mention the bleak nights when he had tossed and turned on his narrow cot bed thinking of the days before he had acquired his deformity, and wanting revenge for what had been done to him. Was this part of the revenge, climbing the hill and seeing the scene of his greatest triumph and disaster? That must be so. He too wanted a clue as to the whereabouts of Lemaitre and it seemed that he had not been too far off the mark. He was astonished to see the large Indian step backwards and reach into his buckskin garment. Bear pulled out a pouch made from skin that hung there from a leather thong that went around his bull-like neck.

'If what you say true, these are yours.' He snapped the string easily with his strong hands and held out the pouch to Iron Hand.

'This could be a ploy just to make me put down my gun,' he said.

'All right, I show you now.' Bear drew open the top of the pouch and withdrew four fairly large lumps of the precious shiny metal. Iron Hand gave a start because he recognized all four, knowing they had been won by the sweat of his brow and carefully counted and categorized with the rest, a couple of dozen in all.

'Those are mine, I would know them anywhere.'

The Indian searched Iron Hand's face for a long moment then put the nuggets back into the pouch and set it down at his feet. He stood up and spread his arms wide. 'For double shame, you kill me now. I die as a warrior, taking punishment for what I have done.' The words were so heartfelt that for a moment Iron Hand almost did as he was told, aiming to put a bullet through the big man's heart and end his misery once and for all. Instead he put down his carbine, lying it on the ground at his feet.

'No, I won't do that. You owe me, Bear.'

The two men looked at each other for a long minute and they must have seen something they both liked because they clasped hands. Iron Hand felt as if he had been caught in some iron vice, and was only glad that by some miracle he had escaped death at the hands of the native.

Without any irony he produced the makings for cigarettes and within a minute or two the men were smoking together while looking over the trees that lined the side of the steep hill, the spectacle of the San Miguel Mountains. They both knew at that moment that whatever else might happen they would remain friends for the rest of their lives. However this wasn't saying much because they were set on a path now that they discussed as they ended their first smoke and lit another. The first one had been in silence; the second was conducted as an expression of their thoughts.

'You're going to have to look for that girl,' said Iron Hand, 'your tribal princess or whatever she is.'

'I do not have the power,' said the Indian, 'the hand of white man turned against my people. If I go investigate, soon will be put in your people's prison or worse.' This was inescapably true. Unless a red man was one of the chieftains and a guest of honour at some ceremony, Indians were not normally welcome on their own. Many people saw them as a threat to law and order. Bear was not exaggerating when he spoke about the result of a lone investigation. Iron Hand sighed, knowing that he had been pushed into a corner.

'I'll help you,' he said. The big man, who was now seated beside him on a fallen log, looked at his companion from the corner of his eye.

'What?'

'I'll help you find this White Dove of yours. Why not? I have nothing to lose now that I've lost everything.'

'You do this for me?'

'No I don't do it for you. I'll explain to you if you want.'

31

'You go ahead. But first let me tell you, I know where they head for now.'

'Where?'

'Denver, he talk many times before he take her away that is where he is going to get us our weapons in return for our help in finding more shiny metal you worship so much.'

'That's a twist,' said Iron Hand. He had started out from Denver, now it seemed obvious that he would have to go back there. 'I'll tell people that we meet that I am a trapper and you're my companion, that I have asked permission of your tribe to employ you in this way.'

'You tell me your story,' said Bear.

'We'll go down this hill and camp for the night, then I'll have a chance to tell you.'

They left soon afterwards, the big man taking the hill in his stride while Iron Hand followed afterwards more cautiously. He did not want to hurt his body any more now that he knew what he was going to do with his life.

He was on a mission.

CHAPTER FOUR

For some reason, now that he had made up his mind to do something about the intruder who had robbed him of his easy life, Iron Hand slept more soundly than he had for many months. This was despite, or perhaps because of the large man who slept in a makeshift tent not far from his own. He had been robbed, but most of the gold must have been used up in one way or the other. He even had some of it back. In his condition many men would have simply given up and found some occupation back in town, and his disability would not prevent him from working with horses or from gambling. Indeed it might be a positive advantage in the latter because other players might be preoccupied with his prosthesis rather than the game, allowing him a positive advantage.

They were many miles from Denver up here in the hills so they would need to go into the town of Columbia – the one that he was sure would end up being called Telluride after the hills.

They caught their breakfast – a hill rabbit that was

not fleet enough of foot to avoid the flashing blade of the Indian. Then Iron Hand put the idea to him.

'Not good for me, Iron Hand,' said Bear, 'many of my kind there helping prospectors, they know of disgrace, might cause trouble.'

'First of all my name is Jake and that's what you can call me, secondly we won't be there for long. We need food and weapons for the ride to Denver if what you say is correct.'

'From now on you are Iron Hand, not as insult,' said the Indian, 'and I can wait outside town for you to get goods then we split them and go.'

The former prospector realized that this was a real test of his new friendship. But he recognized that Bear was quite right to call him Iron Hand because that was the way such titles worked amongst his people. It did not carry the degree of contempt and humour used by the townspeople when he was recovering and going about his business. For instance he knew that this White Dove, when he met her as he was sure he would one day, would prove to be much fairer than many Indian maidens. He knew that such things happened from time to time.

'All right, I'll go in to town and get some weapons, bullets and dried foods for our journey. You will be here when I get back?'

'I wait for you, do not worry.' Iron Hand looked back once. The big man was mounted on his steed, a big Mexican horse that had probably been taken in a raid across the border with that country. Iron Hand nervous that after their sudden amity, the big man might have time to think and would ride off on his own seeking the revenge that belonged to them both.

His worrying seemed to have some foundation. He went into town, used some of the gold (not all of it because that would have been stupid) and came back to the widening of the valley where he had left Bear.

It was empty.

For a brief moment he felt a keen sense of disappointment. Without his new companion he knew that he would never make the trip on his own. Not because of his problems, but because he would need help to pursue an enemy who might or might not have friends with him. He would need the skills of Bear to confront his enemy and deal with him for good. Then, as if by magic the Indian came out of the undergrowth leading his horse. The prospector had forgotten the uncanny ability of his people to melt into the background of any place in which they found themselves. It was one of the reasons why they had been able to resist the incursion of the white man for such a long time even though they lacked his weapons.

'I will take you to hidden pass,' said Bear once he had shared the load with Iron Hand. In effect this meant that he actually carried more since his own mount was so much bigger. 'That way we avoid spying eyes.'

Although he felt the cloak-and-dagger stuff was a bit too much, the man now proud to be known as Iron Hand was ready to go along with his companion. At the very least they were getting towards their target.

The valley was wider at this point and so far they had

met no one else, but Bear took them to the side and found a path between the hills that his ancestors had used as a shortcut for generations. It was known as Barefoot Pass. This skirted the town completely and had the advantage of shielding their progress from anyone who might be watching. The passage was so narrow and rocky that they found it was better to get off their steeds and lead them on foot. This might seem remarkably slow, but they were cutting miles off their journey, which made the effort worthwhile.

'So, you tell me your story now,' said Bear.

'I don't know if I want to,' answered Iron Hand moodily. 'There's not much to it.'

'I listen, OK?'

It was a long time since anyone had listened to him. The doctor was a typical frontier sawbones, who had only been interested in the gold from his patient, and the blacksmith was ready to make the iron hand out of interest in the process, but neither of them had been ready to listen to his tale.

'I came to these mountains because I had been given a gift. The plans were laid out to get gold easily without all the work done by those unprepared fellas.' He told the Indian about his gambling companion and how he had been left a legacy. 'In a strange way, despite gaining, I was doing it as a memorial to Ventman. I could see the work he had put in only for it to be stymied by his bad health. I was kind of doing it for him.' He said these words with sincerity and really believed he meant them. ''Sides, I just hate waste and the thought of gold going begging niggled at me. Seemed to me it wasn't that much of a gamble to come here and give it a go.'

'Then it went wrong.'

'That's the thing, Bear, I didn't know it had gone wrong. When I met that bastard he seemed all right. He's—' he searched for a suitable word '—he's so personable you feel as if you've known him all your life. By the third night, with the cards and a drink or two in us, he found out what I was up to.'

'You told him about the gold?'

'The search for gold was no secret since most people who come to these hills are looking for riches in one way or another.'

'Then what you tell him?'

'You don't understand, friend, it wasn't just a matter of mentioning what I was doing. He had a way with him; he got me drunk, bought the drinks. I think he could sense that I had something the others didn't have.'

'So you show him?'

'No, but I let him help me to the area on Ventman's map. It was a stupid thing to do, but he had been a trapper and he knew exactly where to go to. I paid him for helping me and I thought it was all over when I looked for the exact spot the geology guy had told me I would find.'

'So he not with you when you dig?'

'I'll swear I was always alone. I just think that he was cunning enough to let me do all the work. He left it for five or six weeks. By that time I had made my find.' He could not help letting a note of triumph enter his voice, at which point Mokie made what sounded like a sardonic snicker as if he understood every word that was being said. 'I think he figured that a fortnight would be long enough for me to check out the theory that I had told him while I was drunk. If it was true he would get what he wanted without doing any of the work.'

'So he sneak up on you?'

'I was in the hole I had dug, the one you were exploring, when he turned up. But not with a gun, no, he was much too wary for that knowing that avalanches were common in these parts. No use jumping a claim by shooting someone in the head if two minutes later you were buried under a rush of rock. No, Lemaitre turned up with a stout club made of beech wood and basically clobbered me.'

'But you not stay on hillside?'

'He saw the nuggets I had cleaned and stored in the diggings, and then he attacked me and drove me to the edge. I tried to defend myself and he pulped my hand against a tree. He smashed me over the head and I fell off the steep side of the hill.'

'What happen then?'

'I think he thought I was dead – I nearly was but I had fallen into a clump of bushes. In my head I guess I saw him look at those bushes, then when he saw nothing happen he gathered up all his riches, came down the hills and rode off. That bastard took weeks of my work and just rode off with it without looking back.

'Not that I cared at the time because I was in a terrible state. I drifted in and out quite a few times. Then I remember waking up and saying to myself, "You have a choice. You can take the easy way out, friend, and die here all alone or you can somehow get to the bottom and look for help.'" He paused as he recalled that time. It was hard for him to put the experience into words, but he went on to tell his companion about the long trip down the steep hill towards where he sheltered his mule. It was a trip every painful detail of which was etched in his mind. He had hurt his back and his legs in the fall and his left hand was smashed beyond repair. Several times he had given up hope, deciding that the only thing to do was to lie down and rest for a while. But the sun was beginning to go down and he knew that if he lay down and lost consciousness this time he might never rise again.

Somehow – he still didn't know quite how – he had reached his mule and managed to get on his back. Mokie, sensing that something was badly wrong with his master had stood stock still, his ears back while his master had made several attempts to get on before succeeding in doing so. When they arrived at Columbia town his owner was half dead.

In those days Columbia was a lawless place and one dead prospector wouldn't have made much difference, but fortunately he landed up outside one of the saloons where he had been a regular gambler, along with Lemaitre, before his ill-fated trip. The owner of the saloon, Rueben Smith, who was also the barkeep and general factotum, recognized the man who had slid off his mule only to lie in the cold, hard street. He had taken in the prospector and given him shelter for a few nights. The grateful prospector had used some of his remaining gold to pay for his keep, and for the doctor, whose name was Kenning.

'Turned out it was worth keeping the sawbones on tap,' said Iron Hand ruefully, 'although it didn't seem such good news to me at the time. You see my smashed hand had become infected. You could see the fingers turning a pretty shade of green with gangrene.'

'That must hurt.'

'It did. As the blood supply shut off, the nerves made a blame racket about it. I was in agony night and day. The sawbones – who'd been in the Civil War – made it plain that I had no choice. Either he took the thing off or I was going to die. I remember that day plain as anything. Rueben had me drink a bottle of whiskey, and it was a wonder I didn't die of that rotgut in the first place. Then they put my arm over a table at the side of the iron-framed bed. I was lying on a pine board because Rueben didn't want blood on his mattress. Seemed no point because I was probably going to die. Then, while a couple of townspeople held me down, the doc came with a tool borrowed from the local carpenter and sawed my hand off at the wrist. The blowtorch was already lit. Even through the stupor of the whiskey, it was agony. But even in the middle of my pain I heard the "thump" of my hand hit the sawdust-covered floor.'

'Our warriors would not live with hand cut off,' said Bear. 'They die of shame.'

'Guess so big stuff, but I wasn't no warrior. But worse was to come, I felt the flame searing the wound where my hand had been and I could smell the burning of my flesh – smelled like pork cooking on a campfire. Then he doused it in whiskey – he had been reading about that fella Lister and his fancy ideas about disinfecting a

40

wound – and left.'

'What happen then?'

'I'm under no illusions. The only reason they helped me was because Rueben thought I had an accident and had more gold at my claim. By then he had been given some in the form of a nugget big enough to pay for the whole place. He was keeping me alive so I could tell him the location of my claim.'

'But you didn't?'

'Well it was touch and go over the next few days. I felt like dying, could have turned my face to the wall and said what's the use? I've seen others do it. But there was something in me that said I still wanted to keep going.'

'I understand. My people too call it The Desire, keeps a warrior going in hard time.'

'When I had recovered sufficiently to eat and drink and cover my bones a little I began to brood on the empty space at the end of my arm. It was empty yet not empty because I could still feel my fingers, yet there was nothing there. I've heard of this before, men with a leg shot off who can still curl their toes, but it's all inside here,' he tapped his forehead.

'Everything start up here,' said the Indian, touching the side of his head.

'As the stump at the end of my arm began to heal I noticed most of my wrist was left – there was a reason for that. The doc had noticed that it was my fingers that had been infected and he was trying to preserve as much as he could. So as I lay there I got to thinking. I've seen a lot of men lose limbs or parts of limbs and what's out there isn't much good. You either get a hook of some kind or you don't. In fact I've seen fellas do without the hook because they think it makes them look stupid.'

'So what you do?'

'Luckily, I guess, my right hand was intact and I was able to draw. By then I was already up and doing odd jobs for Rueben so that he had no cause to get fed up with my company. I sat and drew myself a hand with not one, but three fingers, and an attachment at the side that acted like a thumb. The hardest thing was how it would go on to my stump, but I even came up with a leather cup that straps on and holds it in place. I went to the blacksmith and showed it to him.'

'What he say?'

'I guess he was a little bamboozled, never having seen anything like it before, but he was used to making tools and other bits and pieces for the miners and he took on the task, fer gold of course. By that time I had precious little left, but I was starting to earn my keep and I guess I wanted this so much.' He paused and lifted his iron hand up before his face as if seeing it for the first time. 'The fingers are rounded at the tips just like a real hand, and they are jointed, kept rigid by metal stays on the back. There is a reason for this, when I went back to mining I guess I wanted something as flexible as possible. Cost me most of the rest of my gold, but I wouldn't change it for the world.'

They walked on for a while. The pass seemed to get a little easier as it wound through the two parts of the mountain, widening out a little so that they could walk two abreast.

The Indian seemed to be taking a long time to digest

the story that he had just been told and Iron Hand was in no hurry to keep the conversation going. He just wanted to get away from this area so that they could make the trip to Denver.

'You are brave man,' said the Indian finally, 'not kind of Brave who fight just to show he can do in front of others, but kind of Brave who go on and do what has to be done.'

'Thank you kindly sir, it's nice to hear a friendly tone after you nearly killed me.' Iron Hand spoke in a faintly mocking voice, but with a grin to show that he was joking. He regretted the remark the minute it was made knowing that Indians were proud people and did not like being slighted. But Bear had a sly sense of humour and was able to appreciate the irony of the situation.

'You welcome, white man. Lucky you run like rabbit.'

'Lucky you tried the club first and not your blade, big man.'

'True, or you be visiting white man heaven.'

This agreeable banter came to an end a few seconds later as Bear halted his steed and sniffed the air like some kind of animal following a scent.

'What's up?' asked Iron Hand. He knew that the native son would not stop without a very good reason. He trusted Bear's instincts.

'Bad news,' said Bear, 'very bad.'

'What is it, is someone after us? Can you hear other men?'

'No, weather, can you not feel?' Now that it was pointed out to him, Iron Hand realized that the air was distinctly cool, and there was a trace of dampness in the breeze that had sprung up. He also noticed, with some relief, that they were barely 400 feet from the end of the pass. He could see the daylight beyond, his relief tempered by the fact that the pass narrowed considerably so that they would have to go back to single file, as the pass only widened again to about fifteen feet at the entrance. This was a large part of the reason why most of the inhabitants of Telluride did not even know the pass existed. Such paths as these were often weapons that the Indians could use in their fight against the white man, making them able to travel further and faster in their attempts to regain their land.

'I sense a change in the air.'

'Bad, very bad, no time to talk, come now.' Bear grabbed his horse's harness and began to walk at a speed that would have seemed impossible in such a large man. But his feet were clad in thick moccasins and he seemed to sense any rocks at his feet that might make him stumble, avoiding them with uncanny ease.

Iron Hand was not so lucky, he found that if he tried to speed up he began to stumble on the many small rocks and pebbles that were in their way. In addition to this his mule showed his true nature by refusing to go any faster, so that he too could avoid stumbling. Either way, they were both hardly any further along the pass before the thunderstorm swept down from the hills. They were relatively sheltered where they were, but even so the driving rain was so fierce that their clothes were soaked through, and both were freezing cold within mere seconds. However the risk of the cold was nothing compared with what happened next. There was a flash of lightning far above them followed a bare second later by a clap of thunder. There was another flash in quick succession, much closer; the forked lightning struck the side of the mountain close to where they were, causing Bear's horse to rear and whinny. This strike was also immediately followed by a clap of thunder that sounded to their ears like the grumbling of some disgruntled giant.

There was a rushing noise that sounded like a gigantic sigh as the mountain responded to the impact of the thunderous sound and boulders began to tumble down in front of them. They were lucky that the actual pass was so narrow at the top that most of the falling debris triggered by the storm missed it completely – although they had to dodge one or two large stones that fell their way – but most of the rocks, stones and soil landed at the entrance to the pass.

The storm rumbled onwards, soon passing over as they did in these parts, to play out over the great plains of Colorado. The pass was now in semi-darkness because the pile of rocks, stones, soil and pieces of debris that had fallen was piled up to the height of a house in front of the entrance.

They were trapped in Barefoot Pass.

CHAPTER FIVE

A coach came into Denver with some red edging but wearing no particular livery. It had been purchased from a local company for a particular reason, and that reason was concealment. It stopped beside an alleyway and the driver dismounted. He was wearing respectable clothes, with a bowstring tie around his neck and a derby hat like those affected by many in the city. Despite the look of belonging to town life suggested by his clothing, there was an air about this individual that spoke of the times he had spent out in the wilds hunting and trapping for a living. His body was whip-thin and he carried himself with an air of taut expectancy as if he was going to have an encounter of any kind at any minute. The wrinkles around his eyes were the only sign of strain on his pleasant features, for below his neatly trimmed moustache he had a wide, generous mouth. He did not think of himself as a villain, not Claude Lemaitre, for he was a man who was tired of living in the wilderness and wanted something of the better life.

The alleyway was at the side of a large hotel, and it was there that he had arranged to meet the man who would tell him whether or not he had been wasting his time. If he had been, then at least he still had the girl.

He did not spend much time contemplating this pleasant fact. Instead he opened the door of the coach and looked inside. The girl was seated firmly in the interior. She had a large cotton shawl wrapped around her and sat pressed up against the corner even though there was ample room for her.

'I won't be a minute, White Dove,' said Lemaitre pleasantly, 'I need to look for an old friend, and then I can get us on our way. You understand how it is, yes, this is business only. If you waken please do not keep up your struggles, it just causes unpleasantness for all.'

The figure in the shawl made no indication that it had heard a single word. As long as she was not able to move he was satisfied. He made sure that the doors of the coach were firmly secured, and then he went into the main vestibule of the Lomax Hotel. The desk clerk, a boy of barely sixteen, looked at him without much interest.

'I am looking for a Mr Ron Johnson,' said Lemaitre.

'He's in his room,' said the clerk without interest. 'You got a job for him?' he added.

'Why?'

'He's been sozzled three days running is why. If he doesn't pay his bill at the end of the day he's out. Room fourteen.' Since the hotel was not exactly the most auspicious of places Lemaitre reckoned that Johnson would be better off for the deal. He went upstairs to said

47

room and knocked on the door. This was the culmination of a journey that had taken him from living with a Native American tribe to a deal that would make him a helluva lot of money and he wasn't going to be daunted by the fact that he was dealing with a drunken commercial traveller. At his side he carried a brown bag that he had kept low so that the clerk would not notice it. The objects inside made a clinking noise as he mounted the main stairs. The clerk, bent over his copy of the *Denver Sun* newspaper, did not even notice.

As for Johnson, they had first met over a year ago when Lemaitre was staying in Denver and looking at getting into land deals. Trapping was becoming too much for him because he was in his late thirties now and it was a young man's game. Johnson was a commercial traveller for a firm that sold men's clothing and the two of them had met – where else? In the hotel bar where they bonded over a game of faro.

Lemaitre was good at cards, had considered setting up as a gambler, but he knew his own impatient nature and knew that if he was up against an opponent who was better he would start to crack under pressure and that would be his undoing. He could be patient enough when it came to laying traps, collecting his prey and skinning them for sale, but cards were a different matter. People annoyed him quite a lot. He knew this was why he had become a trapper in the first place, that and the easy money it had offered at the time. But taking money from a rube like this on a one-to-one basis was an easy and pleasant occupation. Also, he liked to hear the stories that people had to tell and Johnson, who was in his early twenties and a bright light with the firm, certainly had an interesting tale to tell.

'I come from this area,' he said, 'glad that it became part of the Union in 1876, and Colorado is my home state. Guess it's why they gave me the job out here. It ain't the hardest life, better than what Dad wanted me to do.'

'What did your father want of you?'

'Wanted me in the army, just like him.'

'What about the army? Your old man a sergeant or something?'

'Something like that, he was a lieutenant with Colonel Redmond out at Fort Morgan. Guess life at the fort was different in those days, when a man wanted to bring out his wife and kids it was possible because they would spend years without seeing them otherwise.'

'And you just happened to be one of those kids?' asked Lemaitre. He was keeping his interest to the minimum since he was trying to extract money from the young man and was concentrating on his cards. But it was what Johnson had to say next that electrified him and made him lose that very concentration he was seeking.

'Used to play with a little girl, I was seven and she was about four, mischievous little thing always in and out of our quarters, running around. Cute as a button too. She ripped her dress once when she had a fall and I noticed she had a strawberry-shaped birthmark on her left shoulder. Shame what happened to her and her mother.'

'What happened, *mon ami*?' asked Lemaitre.

'One day a couple of the women decided to take the children out in a wagon for a picnic, they were so bored with being in the fort. I was one of them. Only trouble was, they didn't know that some Utes were in the area and real angry and all at what was going on. You know what them red savages are like. They swooped down on us and put arrows in us, left us all dead, 'cept they took little cutie with them. They did that too you know, used children to negotiate.'

'And what happened?'

'Mister, I had an arrow that went right though me, took me months to recover, nearly died of blood poisoning, but they say that Colonel Redmond nearly went mad with grief over losing his wife and daughter.'

'Ah, my friend, you did not explain that bit. Sore though it is to lose family, for the Colonel to lose such a one to savages must have been a bad loss indeed.'

'The Colonel was – and is – a just man – but he swore that he would kill every Indian he came across for the foreseeable future. He was relieved of his post for a short while until he saw better reason, but they say he is a man who still mourns the loss of his wife and daughter.'

'But did they track down the Utes who carried out the deed?'

'They did, but she was no longer with them, they reckon they killed her and disposed of the body. The cavalry soon disposed of *them*.'

'This Colonel Redmond, he comes from a very good family, does he not, *mon ami*?'

'Why yes, his father is a great land and mine owner in and around this area. They say he could retire tomorrow and live in luxury but chooses literally to soldier on.'

Lemaitre lost the game and retired to his bed shortly afterwards. This was because he had a great deal of thinking to do. In his time as a trapper he had come across a tribe called the Jicarrila. Whatever else the settlers thought of the red man, Lemaitre, like most of the trappers, was a lot more open-minded. The Indians knew their own territories like no other people and they did not mind a man making a living there if he respected their ways. The Jicarrila, living near the San Miguel Mountains for the summer part of the year did not mind him catching the wild beaver and other animals in which he traded, and he had even lived with them for short periods of time. During one of those periods he had come across the strange anomaly of a young woman of about eighteen summers who was dressed like those of her tribe but did not look like them in facial features. Her skin, although darkened by being out in the sun was still fairer than theirs and her hair, although dark brown, was much lighter than theirs too. The facts were clear; she did not really belong to the tribe.

Now that he had met with Johnson and heard the story of that young man, his thoughts then went further. What if the Utes had decided that they could not negotiate with the leaders of Fort Morgan and had passed the child on to the Apaches who also roamed the plains at that time of year? Perhaps the Apaches had meant to use her as their own bargaining tool but had been driven from the area by the onslaught of the cavalry that had killed the original party of Utes? Such things were not beyond the bounds of possibility.

Knowing this, he had returned to the area after meeting and fleecing the young gambler. He knew even then that Johnson was heading for trouble and getting into debt over his gambling, but that was not Lemaitre's problem.

Because there was a real possibility of serious money he decided to take the chance, return to the valley and inveigle his way into the tribe and see what he could do to loosen their hold on the young girl. He had a certain amount of personal charm and he had been able to persuade them that he was going to help them regain their old hunting grounds if he could.

The biggest piece of luck regarding that situation was when he had encountered Jake Holley. Once more, Holley would have been suspicious of a man on the make, but he was willing to open up to a card-playing companion who bought the drinks and had a good listening ear for his woes. The gold he had taken from the luckless miner had been the added bonus that had persuaded the tribe he would use the shiny metal to help them.

In the meantime he had worked on the girl, White Dove. He had quickly established that she did not seem to remember her childhood and considered herself to be as much part of the tribe as anyone. As far as she was concerned she had always been with them. He could understand this; the trauma of being ripped from her parents at such an early age was something she had pushed away as she entered into a new way of life.

He put out of his mind what he had done to get her here. This was too important a situation for him to dwell any more on past thoughts. He paused at the door of number fourteen, thinking best how to deal with the situation, and then he tapped gently. There was no response, so he rapped a little harder and went inside. Ron Johnson was propped up on the bed fully clothed except for his shoes and jacket, the empty bottles at his side telling their own story.

'Mr Johnson, you remember me, it is Claude, remember you told me this is where you stay all the time and I could look you up?'

'Go away.' The younger man opened his eyes and looked blearily at the Frenchman, who was inwardly cursing the situation. This was going to be a lot harder than he thought it would be.

'I can give you some money, help you pay your debts,' said Lemaitre. 'I'm guessing, my friend, that this is why you are hiding inside the bottle.'

'I guess,' slurred Johnson. The mention of money had been some kind of motivation to get him out of his drunken stupor.

'I have a little task for you that will take you hardly any time. But first I have to help you help yourself.' Lemaitre fetched the requisite apparel and deftly rolled the man's socks on to his feet, forced said feet into the shiny salesman's boots and tied his laces. 'We are going for a little walk, my good man,' said Lemaitre grabbing the young man by the shoulders and assisting him to his feet. Johnson gave another groan but began moving along with the older man. After about five minutes of walking up and down the not-too-large, rather flea-bitten room with his companion, he halted and glared at him with red-rimmed eyes.

'You got me Claude, I'm all bright-eyed and bushy-tailed now.'

'I need you to do this one thing for me and I will reward you well.' Lemaitre picked up the brown bag and it gave a few satisfying clinks. 'Just for you to use in your celebrations.'

Lemaitre had already done his homework and took the reluctant traveller down the side stairs where they did not meet anybody, and out into the alleyway. So close, this was to be his time if the truth was discovered. He opened the left-hand door of the coach and found the girl had not moved in all that time. Her stillness worried him for a second, but then he was reassured by the sound of her soft breathing. He pulled the shawl off her. She was wearing a fringed garment of brown buck-skin with straps that tied at the shoulder, but her head was concealed by a silk scarf. Lemaitre signalled Johnson to look into the narrow interior as he sat beside the comatose woman and swiftly undid one of the straps. 'Do you recognize this birthmark?' He asked this as he showed her bare shoulder. There was a pause that was agonizing for the Frenchman, and then the commercial traveller nodded.

'That's the birthmark, the strawberry, then she's —'

'You are sure? What about her face, my friend?' He

pulled the scarf away from her face and turned her head so that she was in profile.

'That strawberry mark, it's the one all right, I remember it from all those years ago. She certainly looks the same in the face, but all grown up. She was always pretty. But that means —'

Lemaitre was already doing up the strap and replacing the scarf. The laudanum would not last forever. He could not give her too much or it might send her to the happy hunting grounds forever, so time was not on his side.

'Come back with me and you will get your reward.' He knew that the young man must have a king-sized headache so he was not surprised when Johnson came back inside and went back to his room through the side entrance and up the stairs. Again they had the good luck not to encounter anybody. It was still morning and things did not generally get moving in a small hotel until noon when visitors were checking in and out.

This one was going to check out without leaving.

'Let us celebrate,' said Lemaitre, opening the brown bag and taking out a bottle of Scotch which he swiftly uncorked. 'Hair of the dog, as you Americans say.' He poured two glasses of the amber liquid and watched with great satisfaction as the young man downed his in one go.

'What about my money?' asked Johnson in a slurred voice.

'I have it here, but first another drink to celebrate your good fortune,' he filled the young man's glass and it was emptied as quickly as the first. A few minutes later the whisky – laced with the same drug he had used on the girl – had the intended effect and the young man collapsed back on to the bed. His breathing became laboured as the combination of alcohol and drugs took hold. Lemaitre did not waste any more time. He pulled the pillow from under Johnson's head then held it firmly on his face, pressing down with all the strength in his sinewy arms. Johnson raised his arms feebly and gave a few muffled cries but within a minute or so he breathed no more. The Frenchman replaced the pillow and the lolling head.

'Au revoir my friend, your debts will no longer bother you,' he said, before slipping out of the building. He made sure that his captive was still held fast in the bonds of Morpheus inside the coach, then urged his horses to pull away from the hotel. If his luck held, the desk clerk would eventually try to deal with the salesman and find his body some time in the afternoon. He would think he had died from the effects of bad liquor – it happened all the time – and that his visitor had slipped out not wanting to draw attention to his presence after finding a body. Again, there probably wouldn't even be a report to the sheriff's office. Ron Johnson had been a nothing.

As he drove to the cabin where he was staying, Lemaitre hummed an old ditty from his homeland.

Life was sweet, and he was going to be rich.

CHAPTER SIX

First of all they had to wait for the shock to die down and their animals to become calm before they decided what they were going to do. A cursory look showed that the entrance to the pass was blocked to a height well above that of a man. Iron Hand turned to the Indian.

'I guess this is where we cut our losses and turn back.' Bear looked stolidly at the mass that blocked their way. The rain had subsided somewhat but his black hair was plastered against his head, only the yellow and green tribal woven band encircling it keeping it in place.

'We not do that.'

'Why not?'

'You not know what path like back there. We lose much time if we return.'

This was so true that Iron Hand did not even argue the point. He stared at the mass of debris that blocked their way.

'I suppose we could try and find a way out of this, but it looks pretty hopeless and we might find ourselves turning back anyway.'

'We have to try.'

Again he knew that the Indian was making a valid point. If they went back to the valley and had to ride through town there was a possibility they could be spotted by friends of their prey and that would never do. Besides, there was a good chance the return had been blocked too. Iron Hand noticed that the Brave had become stock still and was gazing at the debris blocking their way with his head to one side. The former miner knew at once that he was assessing what they should do and there was a look of naked intelligence on the man's face such as you did not often see out here, where the miners and settlers plodded on steadily with their lives. It was a strange thing for him to see, because not all that long ago the very same man had been trying to kill him.

'We dig hole at side,' said Bear, 'let settle then dig some more until we get way out.'

'That might work for you and me,' said Iron Hand, 'but what about the animals, can we make the gap big enough to get them through?'

'We have tools, we do it.' There was something extremely compelling about the big man. Luckily Iron Hand had brought some of his tools with him including a short-handled shovel that had been so handy when excavating in the remains of the extinct volcano, and the Indian had his war axe which was more of a handy tool than anything else because it had a blunt side too that could be used like a hammer to knock rocks out of the way.

The blocked entrance to the pass was the shape of an irregular cookie, about fifteen feet wide. Progress was slow and difficult. Bear man-handled some of the larger rocks out of the way, ignoring the smaller debris that landed on his head, then dodged to one side as a larger boulder rolled down from above and crashed to his feet. If it had landed on his head he would have been killed instantly. He seemed to have an instinct for what he was doing, although much of his success was to do with his prior assessment of the situation. At last he stood back from where he had been shifting the rocks at the right-hand side of the pass.

'Now we dig,' he said.

By mutual agreement they were making the hole as small as possible to cut down the risk of shifting mass. Iron Hand went to work with a will, using his metal hand to balance the shovel while holding the handle and bearing down with his right hand. The stays that held the hand in place worked well and he was soon digging with some of his old rhythm. After about twenty minutes or so of constant work he stepped back, mopping the sweat from his brow. He could see a break in the wall of stones and soil in front of him that showed daylight, but he was just too tired to continue for that moment.

'My turn,' said Bear. He disappeared into the gap and began to shovel with some constraint in case he too brought down the wall of debris. In the worst case scenario either of them could be buried by such a fall and death by suffocation would be inevitable; at the very least, even if they escaped, they would have to start again.

The gap widened and soon he had the pleasure of stepping out to the other side. He looked at the remains of the avalanche that had nearly been their undoing. There was an irregular heap of boulders, soil and even old trees pressing against the pass. He had seen such things before. Most of the mound consisted of soil, and the winter rains would wash it away, clearing the area through natural processes. They just did not have the time to wait for nature to take its course.

Iron Hand took back his shovel and began to widen the gap at the edges. His experience as a miner began to tell, because once the gap was wide enough in his judgement, he packed the earth so that the sides were hard and not loose, lessening the danger of a slide. This meant that they had a fighting chance of getting the animals through.

Time was still a pressure upon them. The storms could return and take their work away in seconds if more debris came down from the mountain.

Iron Hand took the various packs off his mule, which did not look very happy about the whole thing, and took them to the other side, lying them down against a convenient boulder well away from their makeshift doorway. The big Indian did the same with his worldly goods.

Iron Hand went back to Mokie, took hold of his reins and began to lead him towards the gap. Mokie put back his ears, never a good sign, and literally dug in his hoofs. Iron Hand looked at him in despair. At the very worst he would have to shoot his mule and just find a way of continuing without him, but this was something he would fight against with all his power.

'What wrong?' asked Bear, coming through the gap.

'It's this stubborn cuss, he won't shift his mulish ass.'

'You wait, let go.' The big Indian took the reins and then leaned in, whispering softly to the stubborn animal. Gradually Mokie's ears came upright and twitched as he listened to the softened tones of the warrior. Bear walked just ahead and Mokie began to move, finally strolling through the gap and out to the other side. Iron Hand took over and led him to the large boulder.

'What the hell did you do?'

'I tell him much good grass out other side and how happy he be to get it.'

Bear disappeared and Iron Hand watched as he led his own animal through the narrow doorway they had made in the pile of debris blocking the pass. The horse was so big that his flanks brushed the side and he had to lower his head to get through. At last they were together and loaded up their animals.

They were on a trail now that would lead them past the hills and down towards Denver, having cut many miles off their journey.

'I guess our panic was about nothing,' said Iron Hand, looking back at their makeshift diggings. 'We was safer than we thought.'

Even as he spoke there was a gigantic sigh like a man relaxing after a good meal, and the earth shifted downwards, not only sealing away their good work, but covering it to a depth that would have buried them for good.

'The mountain, she laughs,' said Bear.

They rode away in silence.

CHAPTER SEVEN

Lemaitre was in another saloon in Denver, the Pioneer. The town was full of such places, which was convenient for him because he wanted to avoid the hotel he had been at in the morning. This particular watering hole was not the most salubrious establishment he had ever been in, looking as if it was one of the first drinking holes created by the settlers in the 1860s. The exterior sign was faded and the hitching post at the long board-walk was worn and warped and needed a lick of paint, as indeed did the whole of the building. The boards on the sawdust-covered floor creaked as he walked across them to meet the men with whom he wanted to discuss his plans for the near future.

He was leading a busy life because he had little time to waste. Sooner or later the Jacarilla would realize that the girl might have left of her own will, but that something odd was going on. They had had so much taken from them that they would take the loss of their white princess even harder. He had tried to throw the blame on that big Brave who had shown such interest in her, and that seemed to have worked for the moment, but he was not about to become complacent. He knew that events have a way of happening fast.

It was one of those saloons that would normally be empty at this time of day – early afternoon – but the men he wanted to see were there all right, seated at a table playing cards but not seriously, and guffawing with each other.

The Stapely brothers.

'So, it's our little Frog companion,' said the oldest, who was in charge of the other two.

'Hello Tom,' said Lemaitre. 'You are here, as arranged. Are you not going to introduce me to your fine relatives?'

'This here's Wild Bill,' said Tom, 'and the other dead-beat is Jack. You buying us a drink or what?' While he called to the barkeep to bring drinks Lemaitre assessed the three Stapely brothers. They were all from the same mould; tall, rangy looking men with an air about them that said they were not too bothered about keeping within the law. They ranged from their early twenties to about thirty and Tom had a patriarchal air about him, he was in charge and that meant he did most of the talking. Lemaitre did not like the look of them. He had dealt with cowboys such as these before. They were like wild dogs, just as likely to turn on you as help you out.

'I hear that you are able to do something for me,' said Lemaitre. 'I will reward you in a handsome manner, of course.' He sipped his beer. It was warm and slightly flat and tasted like it had come from the interior of an animal quite recently but he tried not to grimace. The others downed their own without any apparent disgust.

'Well, see, that's why we wanted to talk to you, fella,' said Tom. 'You got some money?'

'I have some,' said Lemaitre evenly. He spoke in a low, pleasant voice so that the barkeep could not hear. The man behind the bar though, was keeping a discreet distance. He was well aware of the things done by his more unsavoury customers and he did not want to become involved. 'I come here to make you an offer. You see I have to make a deal and I need your help to make sure that the deal is not – as you may say in English – stymied.'

'And what's in it for us? And what are the details?' Tom snapped the words out, but Lemaitre shook his head. 'There will be thousands of dollars in it for you, but I cannot give you too many details. I want to take one of you with me to help me manage my ward, the source of the future wealth. The other two, I simply want you to keep your eyes and ears open in the town.'

'Then what?'

'If anyone comes near who might cause trouble for me, I want you to make sure that they are no longer any bother.' He took a sip of his beer, not quite managing to disguise his grimace of distaste as it went down. 'In particular I want you to look out for anyone who might be of Indian extraction who is asking for the woman White Dove. Such a person will prove to be of more danger than anyone.'

'You think so, pard?' Tom Stapely gave a harsh laugh and ejected a wad of well-chewed tobacco into the nearest spittoon. 'Guess you don't know about the sheriff we got in this part of town.'

'And who might this person be?'

'Hinkman, Joss Hinkman, that's who. He don't have no truck with Indians unless they prove themselves to be of the tame variety, if you know what I mean.'

Lemaitre did not have to have the term explained to him. A number of Indians, to preserve their lives and that of their families, had taken to Western ways and would dress in the clothes of the white man and take jobs that helped to establish the reach of the settler. These jobs often involved becoming cowboys and working in the cattle industry, or taking employment in one of the bigger ranches. In many cases such people were scorned by those of their own race and were often hated more than the white man himself. The sheriff would have no problem with such people, but it was evident from the words of Tom Stapely that he would see anyone of more obviously tribal roots as potential trouble.

'Well *mon ami*, that is precisely the kind of person we should be looking for.'

'You talk good for a foreigner, but ain't you forgetting something?' asked the oldest brother.

'Ah, you ask the obvious question,' said Lemaitre, 'you settlers, you are very direct people, but I like that, I can work with such.'

'We'll need a small deposit as proof of your good faith.'

'I think I can manage that.' The Frenchman was smiling and easy-going. He did not carry an obvious weapon at his side, unlike the brothers who all wore holsters with identical guns in them – the reliable Colt .45

with six bullets in the revolving chamber. Lemaitre carried a Derringer up the loose sleeve of his jacket and he could bring it into operation in less than a second. If there was to be a time when negotiations were going to go wrong, this was it. There was no real reason why the brothers couldn't murder him for any money he might carry. They wouldn't do it in here of course, since the barkeep was a witness and it didn't do to murder the hired help so you could make a few additional dollars – but they could follow him out and complete the deed if they wanted. Yet somehow the lone traveller did not feel the least bit disquieted by the situation. They needed money and he needed them. He had no intention whatsoever of cheating them, because they were essential to his plans. He laid some bills on the table.

Wild Bill, the middle brother, reached out for the money, but Tom snatched it from under his nose. Bill snarled, but Tom gave him a dark-eyed look and the younger man subsided. Tom got to his feet. Lemaitre was not a small man, but the cowboy towered over him.

'Does it ever get cold up there?' enquired the Frenchman jovially.

'Know what? I guess this is a sign that you're as serious as can be about this deal you're going to make.'

'I tell you, the deal is genuine.'

'And it's worth thousands?'

'Thousands it is.'

'Jack,' said the oldest Stapely, 'get your coat on; you're going away with this gentleman.'

'Aww Tom, I don't want to go and be some kind of glorified nursemaid.'

'You'll go, and you'll do what this gent says. If we get cut in on a deal worth thousands we can set up that ranch we was always talking about.'

'Yeah, but never worked towards,' said the youngest sullenly. He put on his coat and stood by the side of his new mentor.

'May I ask where you are hiding out at the moment?' asked Tom.

'Out at the Wright spread, the old man is out of town for a little while. Your brother will soon find out why. I advise you not to follow us, but to stay in town and carry out your duties as requested. You will not regret doing so. Come my friend.'

The two of them went out of the swinging doors and disappeared. Wild Bill watched them go then turned back to his brother.

'Want me to wait a whiles then go and see where he leads Jack, to find out if he's telling the truth?'

'Naw,' said Tom. 'We got plenty of time to find out about him. Let him go his own sweet way. All we've got to do is find out if anyone comes to town asking about a Frenchman and an Indian girl.' He stretched his arms out and tensed the muscles beneath his blue shirt. 'Don't know 'bout you, but I kind of itch for a bit of action should it come our way.'

'But he's off with Jack, what if he gets this deal – connected with the girl in some way by the looks of it – and tries to double-cross us?'

'Then we gets us some extra action,' said Tom with a wolfish grin. 'But you know, I kind of feel that this one's on the level. I don't get entirely what he's up to, but I think he knows that he hasn't got much time to get the job done – and that's why he needs us.' The two men looked at the still swinging doors. They were as ready as they would ever be, but first they had to dispose of some of that hundred dollars on the best Scotch they could buy.

CHAPTER EIGHT

Although they rode away from the avalanche in silence it didn't take long for the distance to loosen the tongue of Iron Hand. His companion ambled along on his big horse beside the explorer, and would have been able to ride much faster towards their goal if they had both been on similar mounts. However Mokie was big for a mule and his master was light, almost frail, it seemed, so he kept up with the red Mexican horse without too much trouble.

'We nearly died,' said Iron Hand.

'We still here,' said Bear taking it all in his stride. 'The gods have spared us to do task.'

'When we get to Denver I think you should let me do most of the talking.'

'You do that anyway.'

'I'm serious Bear, I know what these places are like. Right now, if an Indian goes about starting what they think of as trouble it won't be long before one or other of us is dead. Or both.'

His companion did not seem too troubled by this thought.

'You talk with your own kind.'

'I'm just puzzled by the fact that you think he took this White Dove off to Denver. Why would he do such a thing? It's a huge distance from the mountains. I don't understand what he wants with her.'

'*He* knows, and that what counts,' said Bear.

They rode on together for many miles. The country-side seemed to roll endlessly onwards and Iron Hand used the opportunity to talk to his companion, noting with interest that the Indian paid a lot of attention to what was being said. The explorer talked about his former life in the town of Denver and how he had gone to look for gold because he had nothing in the town, no family, and no wife, nothing to bind him to the place. As they progressed and Bear responded to his memories, he realized that the Indian was now speaking much better English, ironing out the defects until he was almost fluent with only the odd slip of the tongue to show it was not his native language.

'You see, amongst my people we deal mostly with the Mexicans,' explained Bear, 'and that means that I speak Spanish quite well. My use of your language was rusty because we did not speak a lot to the white man after we were relocated, just the agents who deal with us and the merchants who deliver the cattle under reparations agreements.'

Once more Iron Hand was staggered by the intelligence of the man. To understand and correct the nuances of a foreign language was more than he himself could have done. He had a little Spanish and some French but otherwise could not really master more than one tongue.

'What about Lemaitre, he was amongst your people for months, didn't he speak to you?'

'He used Spanish all the time. As a trapper in the area he found it to be one of the most used languages.'

The night came and they formed an encampment, with Bear once more catching the food, another rabbit, which would see them through. He supplemented this with local roots that he dug from the ground, boiled up over their campfire to make them edible. It rained during the night, so when they got up all they had were some cold remains before setting out again. Iron Hand was in some sort of despair. He was beginning to think that, for him, the trip was a complete waste of time.

'What am I doing? I'm just going back to where I came from, it's all been a waste of time.'

'You want to stay in the mountains?'

'I just think this Lemaitre will have moved on. We'll never catch up with him at this rate.'

'Then we push on. And Iron Hand. . . .'

'Yes?'

'You are wrong.' The Indian spoke with such conviction that Iron Hand took on a new resolve. From now on he was going to go forward and take control of what he was doing. He had a choice, he could let his despair make him turn back and live the rest of his life in relative peace or he could continue and take revenge on the man who had tried to kill him.

'Let's do this,' he said.

Life went on much the same for the next few days. They lived mostly on small game and the beef jerky that Iron Hand had brought with him, while the horses took the ever-dwindling supply of oats they carried and cropped what grass they could. At last they found a trail that was marked out by rocky inclines and passed some minor cliffs, giving them some shelter from the rain that continued to come down intermittently. Soon they were within striking distance of the town.

'You really think he'll be there?' asked Iron Hand.

'I know it,' answered Bear. 'But we do not wait. He will try to spend as little time here as possible. Time is important to us right now.'

'Let's go then.' By this time both they and their mounts were weary from the days and nights spent crossing the plains. Both of them wanted to stable their animals and go find a bed somewhere.

They rode into town, dusty and tired. Iron Hand went straight to a trader where he redeemed some of his remaining gold for money, and then they put their horses into the nearest livery, paying the suspicious owner in advance. The way the man looked at them askance was enough for Iron Hand to think of what they must look like. He decided to hire a hotel room where they could at least retire and refresh before hitting the streets.

They found the Hotel Lomax.

Joss Hinkman was big, standing a shade over six feet in his socks. He was currently walking in downtown Denver. He had a wide set to his shoulders that showed there was plenty of strength to back up his height. He wore dark, sombre clothes except for the red shirt underneath his dark waistcoat, the only colour he allowed, but one that showed a touch of flamboyance in his character.

The five-pointed brass star pinned to his waistcoat was not the only sign of authority, which lay in the way he kept a hogleg holstered on either side of his bullet belt. Many men who had crossed him in any capacity would have attested that these were not there for mere decoration.

Two men were walking down the street towards him. One of them he knew from the past; as an aficionado of the saloons, he had always considered Jake Holley to be one of the drifters in life who would never get anywhere, whose gambling and drinking and the frequenting of the local whorehouse would eventually lead him to an early grave. Not that Hinkman minded gambling, being slightly addicted to the cards as well.

But now there was a purposefulness about Jake that had eluded him in the past. He was also whip-thin, and Hinkman squinted narrowly as he came closer, seeing that there was something wrong with his left hand, the dull metal finally catching his eye. That was a surprise, but even stranger was Holley's chosen companion. Hinkman did not hold too much with Indians walking about as if they owned the place. They were a cause of unrest at times and they could go wild on the local firewater at unexpected moments. He halted in front of the two men on the boardwalk, barring their way with his not too inconsiderable bulk.

'Jake,' said Hinkman, 'I thought you were gone for good, haven't seen you for a long time.'

'Mr Hinkman, ain't seen you for a while,' said Iron Hand.

'Looks like you picked up a friend while you was away.' Hinkman looked insolently over the Indian, while the latter kept a blank look on his features as if he understood little of what was being said.

'Had a bit of luck in the hills,' said Iron Hand, 'struck a little gold. My friend is my personal tracker, hired to help me find more of the same, kind of a good luck charm you might say.'

'What happened to your hand?' Iron Hand looked at this appendage as if surprised that it was present.

'Good luck sometimes happens along with bad fortune.'

Hinkman looked the two men over. Their appearance certainly seemed to back up the words of the prospector. They were both clean and freshly attired. He did not know, of course, that prior to their arrival in the town they had both badly needed to wash and change their clothes. This, along with food, had been their priority when they arrived. Iron Hand had pointed out that they needed to look fairly prosperous if they were going to go around asking questions because no one would give a couple of down-and-outs the time of day. Now they were presentable enough for the job that they had to do and they had not wasted any time in getting on with the task.

'Fine, well I have a few words for you,' Hinkman tilted back his hat and looked at the big man whose gaze was level with his. 'You and Chief Hiawatha here can track yourselves right out of town when you're done with your business. This place is getting cleaned up and you two look as if you're trouble in the making. Do you speak, or are you just dumb?' he added, levelling his gaze at Bear.

'Me not speak much good,' said Bear, 'just tracker for white man.'

'All right, but if I hear about any trouble that happens with your friend here, you'll both go straight to jail.' Hinkman nodded to the men and stood aside to let them go past. He did not like Indians and would have relished doing something bad to the one he had just met, but he was not foolish enough to try it in front of Jake Holley, who had a look of steely determination about him that had never been there before.

'What in the name of Jehosephat was that all about?' asked Iron Hand as they walked towards the first saloon, where they were going to ask a few questions about their prey.

'Your friend does not like my kind,' answered Bear, 'better to act as if stupid with him and let him think he have upper hand than be smart and rouse his anger.'

Iron Hand found that he was in full agreement with this. As long as Hinkman believed he was in control he was easy to handle. Only when angered would the worst aspect of the man come out. Once more the former miner found he was in awe of the intelligence and insight shown by the man walking so calmly beside him.

As he promised, Bear kept in the background while Iron Hand asked the questions. The Indian was met with hostile glances from the barkeeps and some of the clientele, but since he was with Iron Hand they tolerated his presence.

The method of the questioner was plain and simple, he would ask the barkeep if he, or anyone else who frequented the saloon had heard of or seen anything about an Indian girl and a Frenchman having been near the saloon or anywhere in town.

He found that it was easier to do this because he was not a stranger in the town and was a well-known face in many of the saloons. Many who had known him in former times had thought of him as a wastrel and when they saw him return with his exotic companion and a purposeful look in his eye he was offered drinks galore by those who wanted to know his story. In former times Iron Hand would have had difficulty turning down such offers but now he was immune to them, offering his thanks and moving on at the end of every enquiry.

As with many things that took some time, their line of enquiry seemed to come to a dead end and by the end of the day they were both ready to return to the hotel.

'He could be well away with her by now,' said Iron Hand. 'I guess we just lost them. Are you sure they would come to Denver at all? Mebbe this has just been a waste of time on our part.'

'He come to Denver,' said Bear with a look on his face that brooked no argument from his friend. 'Had reason to be here.'

'Well, we'll try one more saloon then we go back and get some shuteye,' said Iron Hand. He meant that they would both get a sleep at the same time because he saw no reason why they had to be on guard. They were the ones doing the searching after all.

The last saloon they entered was The Pioneer. He saw immediately that the atmosphere was different. For one thing although it was filled with drinkers and gamblers and the stink of cigar smoke filled the air, a lot of the men were armed and looked rougher than the clientele of the other places they had seen. This was a place where many dark deeds would be planned. As the two of them entered there was a sudden silence. Iron Hand realized the degree of courage it must take for an unarmed Indian, even one as confident as Bear, to enter such a place where there was not another native face to be seen. As they walked over to the bar he could hear individual protests amongst the clientele and one man even spat at their feet as they walked by. Bear stood by his friend at the bar, arms folded across his chest, an impassive look on his face as once more Iron Hand asked the questions of the barkeep, a weedy man who wore a striped apron.

'I'm looking for some information about an Indian girl and a Frenchman who might have passed through here and left a clue where they were going. There's a reward in it for you.' He expected the answer to be in the negative, as before, but the barkeep looked at him shrewdly.

'I might know something fella, what's in it for me?'

CHAPTER NINE

Weary though he was, Iron Hand did not pass up on the chance that had been thrown their way.

'There's five dollars in it for you.'

'Make it ten and it'll be worth your money.'

'OK.' Iron Hand did not argue with this, he was punch drunk and weary from their long day, and he could always tell the barman to get stuffed if his information proved useless. However this might not be a wise ploy in a place like this that seemed to be full of potential troublemakers.

'I saw a French guy over there just yesterday, talking to a group of men. They was three brothers. They call them the Stapelys. They was having a real good discussion about them helping him, then he left with the youngest brother, Jack. The other two ain't in tonight.'

'Do you know where the younger one and his hirer went?'

'To the old Wright place, far as I know. That's where he leased for whatever he's up to. He didn't make that part too clear and I was a ways away up here pretending to polish glasses.'

'That's all you know?'

'Sure thing. Haven't seen them since they polished off a coupla bottles of my best bourbon. Rats're probably in one of the other saloons, the ones with entertainment if you know what I mean.'

'All right, here's your money,' Iron Hand discreetly slid the note across the counter and the barkeep slid it into his hands. 'We're in room fourteen at the Lomax if you want to send a message.'

'Best if you boys get outta here,' he said, 'lot of people's unhappy that you've brought a native in. They think it kinda lowers the tone of the place.' Iron Hand did not make the obvious rejoinder that the only thing that could lower the tone would be if a fire broke out, since the place was so neglected, but he kept his peace.

'We'll leave.'

They threaded their way to the door. As they did so one man got up and left in front of them. The barkeep saw this, and he knew that Brad Withers, the man who had just left was a friend of the Stapely brothers. He could have called this out and warned them, but it was a hostile place and might start a fight if his clientele thought there was trouble brewing that involved a native. He shrugged and went back to polishing his glassware. They would find out soon enough anyway.

'We go tonight,' said Bear as they walked downtown together. 'Rescue her.'

'I don't think that's a good idea,' said Iron Hand. 'It's late, and they're bound to be on guard against intruders at this time of night. I'd say the chances of getting our brains splattered were quite high.'

'You know this place?'

'Sure I do, it's an old ranch on the far side of town. I'm telling you, if she's still there then they won't be moving out at night, it would be too dangerous for them to go outside town in the dark.'

'This is not our way,' said Bear. 'If we go tonight we get White Dove back and all this finished. I will take you back to the mountains and show you where to get the gold you so long for.'

'And I'm telling you, we're both dead on our feet. We need to get some shut-eye. You're a tracker, you say. We can get them now we know where she is.'

'I do as you ask,' said Bear. 'Truth is I *am* tired and that's when you make mistakes.'

'I promise you, we'll be up real early, refreshed, and do this.'

'I hold you to promise.'

Together they made their way to the hotel.

'What's he doin' here?' The night clerk looked askance at the Indian. 'Manager would've never let him stay if he'd known. Them Injuns are trouble.'

'We'll be on our way soon,' said Iron Hand.

'Make sure you do, I s'pose if there's any bother we're near the sheriff's office,' said the young man.

'I'm telling you, there won't be any trouble, we're just going to grab us some shuteye and get out of here real early.'

'This place always seems to have something going on,' said the clerk as the two men began to climb the stairs, 'hope you don't mind sleepin' in a dead man's room.'

'Ghost stories?' Iron Hand paused at the first landing.

'Nope, literally just the night before you checked in a fella was found dead. His paw was contacted and came to get him. Real upset he was, the paw that is, the fella was beyond anything.'

'That's real bad,' said Iron Hand, turning away.

'Luckily his paw was nearby on business, seems he's going to take him all the way back to Fort Morgan, fer burial that is.' This information seemed to interest Bear, who widened his eyes and gave a nod to his friend. They both came down to the desk and stood on the frowsty rug. Iron Hand looked at the clerk as if he was now interested too, although in reality he was more puzzled than anything else.

'How so, who was his father?'

'Name of Johnson, Lieutenant Johnson, an' he's takin the body out to Fort Morgan to bury him.' Iron Hand saw that his friend was looking at him again.

'How did he die? Was he murdered?'

'No, he was an alky, drank hisself to death, drowned on his own vomit. Reckon that's why the foreigner skedaddled after saying he wanted to visit him.'

'What foreigner?'

'Skinny, wild-looking guy with a real nice smile. Pleasant if you know what I mean. We reckon he must've found his friend dead and decided not to get involved, left by a side door.' The clerk looked at him with interest. He had been trying to spook his visitors because he

82

didn't want an Indian to be staying at the hotel but now he looked with fascination at his visitor's appendage.

'Say, how did you get a metal hand?'

'It's a long story, I'll tell you some other time.' Along with his companion Iron Hand made his way up the stairs and into their room. They had booked one room for two reasons, one being money. They could not afford to waste any. The second was that of security. There was a large bed in the room, obviously one that they could have shared just for sleeping purposes, but as his friend lay down, Bear decided he would take the floor, part of which was covered by a thick rug.

'White man bed too soft for me,' he said.

'Bear, before we sleep, why did you become interested in what that clerk was saying?'

'I don't know,' the Indian shrugged.

'You seemed to know that the Frenchman had been here.'

'Not at all, Iron Hand.'

'It's a strange coincidence that we came to the very hotel he was going to use.'

'Fate happens all the time.'

'I suppose so.' But as Iron Hand settled back on the bed, he had a feeling that he was not being told the entire truth about what the Indian knew, and for the first time since their meeting he felt a sense of disquiet about their companion. He had more questions to ask, but they had experienced not just a long day, but many hard days getting here and it wasn't long before the arms of Morpheus claimed him for their own.

*

83

Brad Withers stood in front of the two brothers. He was in their shack near the stockyards. The two brothers had been neglecting their duties a little, having celebrated the acquisition of hard cash by climbing inside a few bottles each, but now, hangovers included, they were stone-cold sober as their friend alerted them to the presence of strangers in the town.

'Two of them you say?' asked Tom.

'One big Injun, and a guy with a metal hand, staying in room fourteen,' said Withers.

'Guess we should go and see the Frenchie,' said his brother, 'alert him to what's going on.'

'Either that or we go deal with the situation ourselves,' said Tom.

'Where are they based?'

'Hotel Lomax.'

'You sure about that?'

'I trailed them for a whiles just out of curiosity.'

'Thanks, you've been a real help.'

'Well I figured you boys would like to know. Them strangers look like trouble and I knew you were ready to deal with them.'

Withers departed, having done what he thought was his civic duty, and carrying besides a bottle of Scotch with which he had been rewarded for his troubles. He was quite satisfied with this, having run out of funds earlier on in the night when he was still sober.

'Hotel Lomax,' said Tom aloud, 'do you know anything about the place?'

'Sure, it's one of them fleapits in the downtown district.'

'How hard do you think it would be to get into the place?'

'Not too hard, just go there and climb up on the balcony at the side.'

'Seems a crazy way to get in if you ask me,' said Wild Bill, 'but I guess the less people who know we're there the better. You going to saddle up and go over there right now?'

'I don't think so. We wait a few hours, leaving when it's just getting light so it's just dawn when we get there, go in and do what we have to do.'

Wild Bill reached down to his side and drew out his Bowie knife.

'That's good,' he said, 'I've always wanted to use this. Guess it's time for it to be baptized.'

CHAPTER TEN

Lemaitre stood with Jack inside the place he had hired for the duration. The girl was bound up in one of the other rooms. It was the same night when questions were being asked around by Iron Hand and his stolid companion. If word had reached him that this was happening he would have moved her elsewhere because he was jumpy about the situation, but he had some final arrangements to make about taking her to the outskirts of the fort and did not want to leave her on her own after her previous attempts at escape had so nearly been successful.

'You will do as I ask, see that she is ready in the fashion I want. We move out tomorrow.'

'What if she won't do it?'

'Threaten to maim her in some small way. She will not like that, my friend. It is, after all, only a matter of clothes. One more thing. She will say much to you if you let her, do not pay her any attention because she will just be trying to scare you.'

'I don't scare easy,' said Jack, looking a little scared in

86

contradiction to his words. He was out of his depth here. He could be counted on in a fight or playing cards but he wasn't that good at dealing with women having never really experienced much in the way of a one-to-one relationship with any of the fairer sex. He had indulged in some of the tough whores in the saloons but they were not exactly a fair representation of woman-hood.

The old Wright place had been built a long time ago and was a dark, gloomy building with a reputation for being haunted. That was another reason for Jack Stapely to worry about the departure of his employer. He did not want to be left alone in such a place except for the presence of a woman who was sure to hate him for what he represented. The Cyclops lantern on the table cast leaping shadows around the room.

'I have to make a few arrangements beforehand for where we stay,' said Lemaitre. 'I have to meet a man who is letting me use another place near the fort, but far enough away that it will be useful to me. You will be fine, but you must do what I ask. The way she is dressed is not right for what I need.' He departed with a wide smile and a generous nod. Jack was not entirely untutored, he knew what Shakespeare had said about a man smiling and smiling and still being a villain. Beside him he had the bundle of clothes that he was supposed to get the girl into. He was not too bothered at the dress, but he shuddered at the sight of the stockings and the under-garments. Why, he wondered, did her captor not just wait until she was where they were supposed to be for her to change into these? He sighed once more. Again, his was not to reason why. He was going to be paid more for this one job than he had earned in the last couple of years, and that fact alone was enough to earn his loyalty.

Carefully he lit a candle, which sat in a pewter holder, and then went to the door of the room in which the girl was being held. The door had been locked with a large key, and he turned this, hearing it click in the lock while the candle guttered in his hand as a draught tore through the old building. The girl was in the corner, hands tied behind her as she lay on an old horsehair sofa, still dressed in her buff fringed garments. He had to say that she was a wonderful looking woman, with long, shapely legs and a face that when it was in repose promised all sorts of delights for any man to whom she might be attracted. He sat the candle on the windowsill opposite, and then approached her with the bundle of clothes under his arm. Her eyes remained firmly closed.

'Miss, missy.' He did not know her name. Lemaitre had deliberately neglected to tell him this. He sat the clothes at the other end of the sofa and untied the gag around her face.

'What do you want?' her eyes snapped open and she glared at him.

'Miss, my name is Jack, I have been hired by Mr Lemaitre. He wants you to change into these here duds.'

'Does he, Jack?' The girl struggled upright on the sofa and looked at him calmly. 'Jack, will you do me a favour?'

'No missy, I can't be doing you any favours.' He stepped back, with his gun in his hand. 'I'm just asking you, real reasonable like, to put these on.'

'Jack, you are party to a kidnapping. Do you know what they do with kidnappers? They put them on a platform and stretch their necks with a length of hemp.'

'If I untie you, you'll be putting on the clothes.'

'You're a handsome young man Jack, but I can just see your mouth in a rictus of death.'

'Stand up; I'm goin' to untie you.'

'Jack, Lemaitre is a lunatic. You're being drawn into his schemes. Even if you don't get hanged, you'll all be dead within days.'

'Stand up, turn round.' The girl stood up as asked and turned around. He used one hand to untie her while he held the gun in the other. As the bonds dropped away he stepped back so that he was well away from her. She turned around rubbing her wrists. She suited her fringed dress and her deerskin boots. Indeed she was so shapely that for a moment his mind strayed from his duties. The girl saw what was on his mind and smiled at him.

'It wouldn't be hard for you to kiss a pretty girl, would it Jack? You are not unattractive you know.'

'No, I will not kiss you, now get these duds on.' Jack knew that he found the woman attractive, but he was also certain that he did not want to displease his elder brother. 'I'm going to wait outside and lock the door. Now get it done.' He backed out of the door, still pointing his gun at her, then quickly slammed it behind him and turned the key in the lock. He stood there for a few minutes trembling with a mixture of disgust and lust.

'I'm ready,' said the girl from inside the room. He

89

unlocked the door cautiously and stepped back expecting her to launch an attack on him. He knew these Indian women could be like that – but instead he found her standing dressed in the garments that had been bought for her by Lemaitre. She looked the epitome of wholesome womanhood, her discarded native clothes lying in a corner unwanted.

'Well, Jack, what you think?'

'I think you look – you look like a woman who could be living in this town.'

'Well that's a real compliment for a lady. You're saying I look ordinary.'

'You could never look ordinary.'

'I figured I could resist your demands to dress up and look pretty or I could just do what you asked. Since I don't mind looking good I decided to put on these clothes. Besides, there's another reason why I did this. If I look like one of your women, when I escape it will be much easier to get help from your people.'

'Stop talking like that!'

'Besides, I was engaged in a sort of way to a member of my tribe, he will be looking for me now. When he finds me he will kill you with his war club and your brains will go flying.' For a second she dropped her pleasant face. 'I think I'd like to see that,' she snarled.

'Turn around.'

'Why?'

'I have to tie you up again.'

'And if I disobey?'

'Then I'll have to knock you out with my fist.' He did not like threatening a woman, especially one as pretty as this, but he had a feeling that she was not going to be a walkover.

'All right.' She turned around.

'Put your hands behind your back.' She did as he asked and he bound her arms, using an initial loop in the rope to secure her wrists together and only putting his gun down when he thought she could not break free so that he could use both hands to bind her more tightly.

'Makes you feel good does it, treating a woman like this?' she asked calmly as he continued with the process, and then proceeded to call his lineage into question suggesting that perhaps his father was not legally bound to his mother and that, in addition, that parent was probably his father's sister.

'Shut up,' he cried at last. He gagged her and flung her on the old horsehair sofa. He left the room trembling still with lust and fury. If she had not been the possession of Lemaitre he would have showed her there and then what he thought of her because she had so angered him; he would have violated her. He locked the door and stood against it waiting for his fury to die down. Thank the Lord they would soon be getting rid of the bitch. He got himself some shuteye in one of the uncomfortable chairs the place had to offer. The first light of dawn began to steal through the windows as Lemaitre returned, but this time he had something with him.

CHAPTER ELEVEN

In the meantime, just before dawn the two brothers rode their horses down the street in a manner that could only be described as furtive, at a slow pace and keeping well in the shadows. They got off their steeds well before they got to the hotel. Hitching their horses to a nearby rail, they made their way down to the side of the building. On their way they noticed there was a light burning in the vestibule of the hotel. This was where the young night clerk was quietly dozing over the curled pages of his local newspaper.

'I guess they won't lock their door,' said Tom, 'means they can move out quick when they need to.'

It was still dark, but there was enough light from the threatening dawn to show where they were going. They knew that the side door would be locked, but they were young and fit. The hotel had a kind of walkway around the outer edge with a balcony that had gaps at intervals. Empty water barrels stood at the side of the building and Tom climbed atop one of these, grabbed the edge of the walkway and pulled himself up. He reached over the edge and helped his brother to do the same.

For a moment they stood on the walkway to get their bearings, and then they went to the long windows on their side of the building. These opened outwards and were left slightly ajar in the hot weather to let some air into the hotel. These were pulled wide with hardly a creak and they let themselves into the corridor beyond.

It was strange how sounds that would go unnoticed during the day were magnified to a gigantic extent at night. The pair winced with every step that they took as the creaking floorboards threatened to betray their presence.

They were just two shadowy figures in the darkness now, but Tom had come prepared and lit a lucifer which flared with just enough light to quickly let them get their bearings. They saw the legend '14' just next to where they were standing. Tom dropped the spent match and drew out his knife, with Wild Bill doing the same.

'Remember, this is for the ranch,' he said, bolstering his courage, and pushed the door open.

That was just the beginning of their troubles.

Iron Hand was in the middle of a dream where he heard the rumble as an avalanche threatened to descend upon him. His senses had been honed to a fine point since he had lost his hand so that even the faintest noise was liable to awake him. The bed had been comfortable enough, but the mattress was stuffed with horsehair rather than feathers and not as soft as Bear imagined, so when there was an intrusion he was alert to what was happening and instantly rolled to one side and on to the floor rather than springing out of bed. This was a good thing to have done, for if he had sprung forward his throat would have met the point of a sharp knife and this would have ended his life in a welter of blood. As it was, the shadowy attacker could not halt his momentum and his blade slashed and embedded in the pillow on which Iron Hand's head had reposed just seconds before.

Dawn light was just starting to filter through the curtained windows as Iron Hand got to his feet. He knew that his attacker would not be off balance for long, so he lunged at the dim figure and launched an attack of his own. He was now behind the man who was just about to free the knife and brought down his left hand, using it as a club. The man gave a grunt of pain as the metal made contact with his skull and slid to one side, stunned by the blow.

In the meantime Bear had been busy. As the second intruder came through the door the Indian reared up behind him and grabbed at his arm. But Wild Bill was slicker than his more solidly-built older brother – he twisted his body away from the defender and swung his knife upwards in an arc which would have opened up the abdomen of the other man if it had made full contact. As it was, Bear thudded against the wall and a slash appeared in the front of his tan jerkin.

Wild Bill, not so wild as his name suggested, saw his brother go down and immediately retreated out of the open doorway and into the corridor, closely followed by the man whose life he had tried to end.

'Who send you?' asked Bear, reverting to a more primitive form of English under stress. The answer was another wild slash from the knife. Then Wild Bill saw something in the Indian's hand that sent a chill thrilling up his spine. It was a short-handled war axe which Bear had snatched up as he followed this new enemy out of the doorway.

'It was the Frenchie, he told us to get you,' said Wild Bill. He turned and ran towards the double doors that led to the outside of the building, closely followed by his enemy. Bear had no intention of killing the man and just wanted to capture him so that they could make him give up more information, but the younger man made the mistake of turning around as he was pursued and smacking his opponent in the face. A kind of red mist descended over the Indian and he gave a roar that seemed to shake the building to its very foundations. He now thought about nothing but destroying his enemy.

Downstairs the night clerk heard the commotion and did what any sensible person would do in the circumstances. He fled out of the building and ran away as quickly as his short legs would carry him, only looking back once he was a safe distance from the hotel. What he saw was a sight that would have frightened any reasonable man. A big native, his face contorted in rage was confronting a cowboy on the narrow walkway that surrounded the building. Outlined against the new dawn, he seemed like a menacing giant, bigger even than the man he was confronting. Worse still, in his hand the Indian held a war club which he was raising menacingly above his head. The clerk gave a cry of fear, turned away from what would be the inevitable end, and ran to find the sheriff, who was stationed nearby.

What the clerk had not seen was the way when they were still inside the building on the verge of coming out, that Wild Bill remembered that he still had a gun and drew it out of its holster to shoot his attacker. Neither of the brothers had wanted their presence here to be known. Indeed they had wanted to leave two wordless corpses who would be discovered hours later. But this was a situation where a bullet might save him even if it did lead to complications further down the line when the law became involved.

However this did not work out as he planned either, because the Indian reached out a hand that could have crushed walnuts and swatted the gun out of Bill's nerveless fingers as if it was a toy. The weapon clattered harmlessly to the ground so that he was forced to retreat out on to the walkway. He could have saved his life even at this late stage if he had thrown up his arms and surrendered, because there was a shout from the inside of the building as Iron Hand ran into the corridor and appealed to Bear.

'Capture him, he'll be useful to us.' This might have been good advice, but Wild Bill still carried his knife. In his panic he had forgotten about his remaining weapon and slashed out again, wounding his opponent on the arm. Bear gave a roar of pain and raised his war axe at which point his opponent fell off the roof and on to the dusty street below. Bear, carried forward by his own momentum fell on top of the man, feeling bones crack as his own fall was broken.

In the meantime Iron Hand heard a noise behind him. He turned to see the older brother who had obviously been temporarily stunned, rushing out of the room. Iron Hand cracked him on the side of the head again. Disoriented, but trying to help his brother, Tom ran forward out of the long windows and was carried forward so fast that he too encountered the balcony, gave a scream and fell on to the street below.

Unfortunately he collided with the edge of the walkway and there was a horrible cracking sound so that he lay there, staring into space, with his head at an unnatural angle because of a broken neck.

Bear got to his feet, weapon still in hand and looked contemptuously at the corpse of the man who had tried to kill him. A rifle shot kicked up the dust at his feet. Still with war axe in hand he looked up to see that Sheriff Hinkman was standing there with a still smoking Winchester rifle aimed straight at the victor.

'Now, Chief Warpath, put your toy down or I'll drop you where you stand.' Just a few yards away from the sheriff stood the clerk who looked both excited and frightened in equal measure, having completed his task.

'You got him, Sheriff, you sure got him,' he babbled, looking with horrified fascination at the corpses.

The victor wanted to live to see his task fulfilled so he did as he was asked and dropped his weapon to the dusty ground. He looked around at the same time to see where his friend had gone.

A whole group of people who had been sleeping peacefully in the building, including an old man in a red flannelette nightgown and a lady in a blue dressing-gown were gathered at the front of the building commenting in various tones of outrage and annoyed enjoyment. But of Iron Hand there was no sign to be seen. He had vanished with the morning sun.

CHAPTER TWELVE

When Jack heard the noise at the front door of the Wright place he awoke from his shallow slumber with a gasp. He made his way to the door expecting to see a person who had completed his negotiations. Instead he found a lithe Frenchman standing with a large box full of God-knew-what.

'Don't just stand there!,' said Lemaitre testily. The young cowboy hastened to help his new master and took the goods inside. Lemaitre checked inside the box and Jack was astonished to see it was filled with photographic equipment, including a bellows camera, camera stand, and a sealed black box that must contain the photographic plates, a powder flash gun and a container of powder for said accessory. Jack gaped at the equipment.

'What the hell?' he asked no one in particular.

'I had to pay much for the use of these things,' said Lemaitre. 'Come, do not have much time.' He went with Jack to see their prisoner, whom the young man untied. She was already awake and they allowed her to walk up and down until the stiffness in her body abated. 'Now there is a task we must complete,' said Lemaitre.

'Well I have a task too that involves going somewhere,' said the girl, 'unless you want me to spoil these fancy duds.' The Wright place did not have elaborate sanitation facilities, so they accompanied her across the backyard to the thunder house – a modest wooden faintly green box forty feet from the building. Being right on the edge of town the ranch was hardly overlooked by neighbours but the two of them kept an anxious eye out for the girl until she had finished what she needed to do and came out.

'Lucky there was a Sears in there,' she said. 'You white men have some good things after all.'

Jack could not understand why the girl did not seem to be more upset. The two men were more nervous than she was. The two men got her inside and Jack covered her with his pistol while Lemaitre set up the equipment with suspicious ease. White Dove's only objection seemed to be that she did not have a comb for her hair, but since it fell naturally away from her face and was not too curly, she smoothed it with her hand and everything was fine. Lemaitre got her to look at the camera, inserted the plate and operated the flash. Jack started at the minor explosion and the bright light and nearly tightened his finger on the trigger, which would have ended his duties right there and then.

'Now turn around please,' said Lemaitre, 'I need to do one more thing.' He pulled down the top of the dress so that it exposed her birthmark.

'My betrothed is going to kill you both,' said the girl

in a conversational way as she turned her back to them. Jack was white-faced at this. To him it was obvious that she knew something he did not, but Lemaitre merely smiled.

'That may be so, but we have to operate on the basis that this will not happen.' He operated the flash again. 'One more to the front in case anything goes wrong,' he said, and this was done. He packed the equipment away with an air of a job well done, carefully wrapping the photographic plates so that they were not exposed to the bright light that filtered into the room.

'Make sure she is fed and watered, she must be in tip-top condition,' said Lemaitre as he left the two of them together. 'I must take this equipment into town and get the photographs developed. I have also my deposit to get back, and even then it took some persuasion for him to let me do this; as you say in these parts, no rest for the wicked.'

'No,' said the girl, 'just a bullet in the vitals.'

Once the Frenchman had departed the girl looked at her companion with scorn writ large on her pretty features. She really did have the most spectacular eyes; Jack felt his knees go weak although he countered this with a stern face.

'Well,' she said, 'you heard the man. Feed me.'

CHAPTER THIRTEEN

Putting his hands to his head so that they covered his face, Bear sat on the wooden bunk that could hardly contain his great frame and looked at the ground. He was in a state of mind that his tribe would have recognized. He was ashamed of having surrendered to the sheriff. The only reason he had given in was because he still had it in his mind that he would be able to rescue White Dove if he could get away from here. They had been so close to finding her and it had all been taken away in a minute.

Intermixed with the shame was a terrible rage directed against Iron Hand. Just when he thought he had made a real friend in a white man, that friend had turned out to be as false as the rest. They made promises and assurances that they did not keep. Like his people he was a straightforward, simple man, who believed that you should do what you said you were going to do.

He was in the jail at the bottom of the sheriff's office. He had already been told by Hinkman that he was going to go on trial for murder and that given he was already one of those troublesome natives who were trying to halt progress he would probably be lynched.

'In fact I would do the job right now,' said Hinkman in a friendly manner, 'you want to try and escape right now and I'll shoot you dead? That way you don't have to go through the formality of a trial and we save the County a lot of money.' He looked at his prisoner more thoughtfully. 'On second thoughts, releasing you from your chains might not be a good idea, 'cos you look as if you could cause a mighty lot of damage before you were brought down.'

'We fight man to man.'

'Sorry boss, that ain't an option. Now you stay in your cell real quiet and we'll see to you in the morning.'

Now it was heading towards the afternoon. The sheriff had already been out gathering some evidence, and then came back at dinnertime having already eaten in one of the local cafés. After that he had brewed some coffee on the potbellied stove in the corner and sat back in his chair, eventually slumbering and snoring through his thick grey moustache. He had two deputies who patrolled the town, and since most petty crimes went unreported anyway, they were enough to keep order in the meantime.

At this juncture there was a knock on the door. Bear did not uncover his eyes, but remained in exactly the same position. The sheriff tried to sleep on but the knocking continued until he got up, rubbed his eyes and flung the door aside only to discover an unexpected visitor before him.

It was Iron Hand.

'Hello, Sheriff Hinkman, can I come in?'

'What do you want?'

'Oh it's Jake here, purely a social visit. Thought we could have a chat and a game of cards.'

'Come in.' The sheriff did not hesitate, but stood aside for the new visitor. He looked carefully but Iron Hand did not seem to be armed. This did not fool him for a moment. He knew that it was easy enough to keep a pistol in a pocket or even a concealed holster under the arm. However in the case of the miner, he did not think there was any such deception.

'Coffee?' The sheriff poured two cups of the strong black brew and brought them over to his desk, at which his visitor had seated his butt on the spare seat.

'Thanks.' Iron Hand drew out a deck of cards and spread them on the desk. 'A little game of faro, Sheriff?'

'Sure, why not?' They played in silence for a while, even drinking a couple of cups of coffee. The stake they played for was just a couple of dollars. Hinkman won both times, although whether by luck or good judgement it was hard for him to tell. He knew that Iron Hand had earned money from his gambling in the past, so he could have been just trying to soften up his target. While he was concentrating on his cards, Iron Hand used his prosthetic appendage to make one or two subtle signals to the man in the cell.

It was wonderful to see the transformation that had taken place in the big Indian. On hearing Iron Hand's voice he had lifted his head from his hands so that he was able to see what was happening. On the acceptance of the game of cards he had leaned his body forward, tensing his muscles, ready for action. His face had remained completely impassive as was the way of his people, but there was an expectant air about him that had not been there before.

Hinkman leaned back in his chair and looked impassively at Iron Hand.

'I know why you're here of course.'

'And why am I here, Sheriff?'

'To secure the release of your friend, of course.'

'You saw us together, so I won't deny that there is a connection between us.'

'He's only a lousy Indian. You can pick up another guide quickly enough.'

'I've kind of got used to this one, if you want to know the truth.'

'Well, get used to being without him. He'll go on trial tomorrow and before sundown he'll be stretching his neck on the gallows. Reckon we'll get a pretty good turn out. He's a big 'un, strong. He'll take a good long time to do his final dance.'

'Sheriff, did you know the two dead men?'

'I sure did, the Stapelys. There's a third one but there was no sign of him at all.'

'Then you must know their reputation.'

'Sure I do,' said Hinkman imperturbably. 'They're a – sorry, they was a – bunch of the lowest you could get. They was arrested more times in a year for drunkenness and general criminality than they was out free.'

'Then you'll know that I'm not asking for much. Look into the situation, that's all. What were they doing at the hotel, why did they attack people there? Ask the clerk, Jem, he'll tell you that they must have been in the building in order to fall from the walkway. How did they get in? He certainly didn't let them through the front door. Ask him about the state of the room this man was staying in.'

'I'm listenin'.'

'Above all, look at the corpses of the two men. There isn't a mark on them except those caused by the falls that they made.'

'There's an awful big mark on one of 'em where that one over there fell on top of him. Broke his fall but didn't help the other fella much.'

'Yep, I guess so, but look at the facts. He's the only one who has any wounds caused by a direct attack. Wouldn't you say it would be reasonable to think that he was defending himself against two attackers who had decided for some reason that they were going to kill him?'

'You could look at it that way, I guess, but see here son, the process of the law is what matters here. I know those worthless dirtbags was up to no good. You stick around and we'll put that fact in the court.' He looked sharply at Iron Hand. 'Come to think of it, where was you when all this was happening?'

'I was around,' said the other. 'That's not the point. I'll tell you the whole truth, Sheriff. We're looking for a girl.'

'A girl? Mighty strange way to go about it if you ask me, that leaves corpses littered all over the place.'

'I'm talking about a girl who was taken from her tribe by a man who is using her for his own ends.'

'Why didn't you come to the law sooner then?

Kidnapping is a serious business.'

'Because of who she is and because of who we are,' said Iron Hand bluntly. 'We all know the law is not equal.' He stood up and went across the room towards the three cells at the bottom of the office. There was only one occupant to be seen, his friend, who was still in chains and who seemed like a statue was sitting there. 'Look, Sheriff Hinkman, you've known me for a long time. Let this man go and we'll work together to bring back the real miscreant.' He did not have any real hope in his voice.

'Son, I can't do that.' The sheriff stood up and walked towards his opponent. 'Come to think of it, I reckon you should put your hands up right now.' He took out the hogleg from his right-hand holster and pointed it at the former miner.

'What? I don't understand.' As he spoke, Iron Hand deliberately closed the distance between them and moved closer to the bars of the cell. Hinkman was so caught up in what he was doing that he followed almost automatically.

'I said put up your hands. I reckon you was there and you was involved in the killing of those two men. Now make another false move, I'll shoot. I won't kill ya, just wound you enough to disable ya, the court doesn't care if prisoners have resisted.' He was a little complacent because he was dealing with an unarmed man. As he said this, Iron Hand gave an almost imperceptible nod and the sheriff found himself being dragged by a strong hand towards the cell that held his prisoner. He quickly turned to counter this by using his gun and shooting the offender. As he did so, Iron Hand sprang forward and thudded his metal fist into the side of the lawman's head. Hinkman immediately became limp. Iron Hand's weapon had been in plain sight the whole time. The Indian, unable to hold his weight, let go of the sheriff, who ended up sprawled out on the ground. Iron Hand did not waste any time. He took away the sheriff's weapons and grabbed at the keys that descended from his belt, moving quickly and decisively. There was a reason for this; he knew that the sheriff had two deputies and that they could come back at any time.

Within a minute he found the key that let out the big Indian. He spent another few precious seconds undoing the chains that held together his feet and his arms. The Indian gave a satisfied grunt and walked about to try and restore his circulation, then assisted Iron Hand in dragging Hinkman into the cell. They had the presence of mind to use material from the blankets to gag and bind him. The cell door clanged behind him and the man who had tried to take away their freedom was as much a prisoner as they would have been, only without the prospect of a trial.

'I'll make sure the coast is clear enough for us to slip out.' The smaller man looked to either side. The sheriff's office was shaded by a veranda roof for the hot days when he might want to sit out. This, and the fact that not too many people were around allowed them to slip out unnoticed.

Although he did not know every street, Iron Hand had a gambler's ability to recall exact details. He could see in his mind's eye exactly were they should be going.

Soon they were at the livery where they fetched their mounts and headed out to the Wright spread.

'Where were you?' asked Bear.

'I didn't see much point hanging around when you were fighting those two idjits, especially when that dopey clerk went for the sheriff, so I went off and prepared for a flight away from his clutches. That's why all our stuff was waiting here for us.'

'You came back for me?'

'I had to. Otherwise this whole thing would fall apart. I need you, Bear.'

'Thanks.'

The two men rode off in silence.

CHAPTER FOURTEEN

Lemaitre arrived back at the ranch in good spirits. It was still early in the morning. 'Time to go,' he said. 'Everything is prepared. Get the girl and we will depart hastily.'

'What about my brothers?' asked Jack. 'Do they know where I'm going?'

'Not precisely, but I did give them a general outline of what I was going to be doing.'

'I wouldn't mind speaking to them before we leave for this place – where is it?'

'Once more, I will tell you on a need to know basis *mon ami*. Sufficient to say that the trip will take several hours and we must leave now. What else am I paying you for but to do as I ask?'

This was enough to galvanize the other man into action. Once more they got the girl into the interior of the coach. She resisted their efforts passively since her arms were bound, and the dress was sufficiently long that it prevented her from kicking out at them. All the same, she was a dead weight and it was a sweating and cursing young man who finally sat across from her in the interior. Lemaitre was not with them. He wanted as few people as possible in on his plans so he took on the role of coach driver, a task at which he was proficient, having handled many animals in the course of his life. Most of them had been dead, of course, because that was the way he had made his living, but he had used horses for most of that time and he was certainly not about to tell all to his aide, who was simply there because he was needed.

Lemaitre had also failed to tell the youngest brother the knowledge that he had gained just before returning to the ranch. The photographer – Mr Jameson, from whom he had borrowed the equipment (for a hefty sum far more than its value plus a deposit) – had chatted with him while the prints, now tucked safely away, were being prepared.

'That is a terrible affair, just downtown.'

'What?'

'Two young men have just been brutally murdered.'

'What?'

'They were killed by a marauding Indian, a big beast of a man, leapt on them in a hotel. Went berserk and tried to scalp them. They were brothers, the Stapelys, a nasty pair of rogues, but still, what a terrible thing to happen as a new day dawns.'

This was information that Lemaitre was keeping to himself.

Jack, however, was not as untutored as he seemed. He

had relatives in some of the far-flung districts and he had been this way before. From time to time he looked out of the window at the passing landscape and articulated where they were going. It was an unfortunate trait of his character that he had to speak his thoughts aloud.

'Northglenn,' he said at one point. 'Keensburg,' a great deal later, with other, smaller settlements mentioned in between. 'I know where we're heading,' he said at one point, 'Fort Morgan. Well I'll be the son of a bush porcupine. What the hell is the Frenchie going to do at a military installation? You'd think he'd avoid the place instead of going to it.' He was not a deep thinker and did not seem to consider the effect his words would have on other, listening ears.

One thing he had done, though, was to take pity on the girl. It was warm in the interior of the coach and there was no need to keep the gag on because of the rattling of the wheels. It was even doubtful at times if they could hear each other, although he did not know that the sharp hearing she had developed with the tribe still enabled her to make out the place-names he was saying. The upshot was, he removed her gag and made her bonds more comfortable.

'Thanks,' she said, 'I might not put a knife through your heart after all.'

'This trip is taking longer than I thought it would,' said the young man. 'We'll have to stop for the obvious break at some point.'

'I hope so, or you're going to be sorry for the rest of the trip.'

As he predicted, they halted and he had to take her

into the undergrowth for her to relieve herself. By that time they had been travelling for several hours and the sun was already well up in the sky. Jack waited while she went into the bushes to do her business. She rounded on him as he followed her.

'Are you going to watch cowboy, is that how you get your kicks?' With flaming cheeks he had pulled back and given her some privacy.

The roadside at this point was quite heavily forested. After several minutes he heard the sound of undergrowth being crushed – but in the opposite direction. He suddenly realized that the girl was not as passive as he had thought. She was clearly attempting to escape. He cursed himself for being a fool – he had even untied one of her hands for more obvious reasons.

Fortunately for him luck was on his side because in her haste to escape she had fallen over a wind-blown branch and lay sprawled on the ground. As he helped her to her feet she used a few well-chosen curse words that showed she was well-versed in the English language. Fortunately for him, the area was dry and she had fallen amid some large springy ferns so her dress was practically unmarked. As he marched her back to the coach a cold sweat broke out on his brow at the thought of what his employer would have done to him if she had escaped, or her dress had been damaged.

They got her back into the coach without too much force. Once more the fight seemed to have gone out of her, while her captor was still digesting the enormity of what had nearly happened. Lemaitre had spent a lot of time and money on her. If she had gone missing there was a very good chance he would have turned on Jack and killed him right away.

This time they did not stop until they were a couple of miles from Fort Morgan. There was a town of the same name signposted in front of them, but the driver took a left fork that led into wilderness until he came to a spread that made the Wright place look shiny and new. It was a deserted homestead with a fence in a poor state of repair and a roof that suffered from some kind of dry rot. They managed to get the girl inside. The place had some rudimentary facilities and it was better than some of the places Jack had lived in with his brothers.

Jack carried in the rest of their belongings – which mostly consisted of food.

'There's a stream nearby where you can be getting water,' said the Frenchman. 'Take care of her, since I may be gone for a few days. If you harm her in any shape or form you will have me to deal with.' He said this in quite a soft voice, which made the threat all the more chilling.

'I'll do what you want. But where are you going?'

'The less you know the better. You will see me in a few days when I will be a very rich man and this filly will be ready to leave us. Then you will be richly rewarded.'

'And my brothers too.'

'Ah yes, the brothers. That too, *mais oui.*'

If he had not been worried about the near future the young man might have caught an odd inflection in his master's voice at the mention of his brothers. Lemaitre unhitched one of the horses that seemed in good condition, after the coach was hidden out of sight in an old outhouse, while the rest were turned out to graze, and turned his face towards the town. As he rode off into the distance the young man watched him go with a strange, leaden feeling inside, then turned and went to see to the girl.

When Iron Hand and Bear reached the old Wright spread on the edge of town it was as empty as they had predicted. Bear had dismounted well before getting to the main building and proceeded to stalk around the ranch in a way that argued he had done this kind of thing before. His friend was much more direct and looked around at the trail leading from the building.

'No one here,' said Bear.

'How do you know?'

'I can just tell. Hard to explain to you. Anyway you see the marks of the coach. They left here hours ago. We must leave too.'

They hardly needed to discuss why they had to go. They had little in the way of supplies and their money was running low, but also the sheriff would soon be found and after that their lives wouldn't be worth living. They would be hunted down by a posse, and since they had committed a jail break there was every good chance that they would be lynched there and then. Once out in the wild country their chances of staying alive increased dramatically.

'Only thing,' said Bear, 'you have to lose the mule.'

Iron Hand knew that a lot of how he felt was tied up in Mokie. This was the animal that had saved his life, but sturdy though he was, his main drawback was speed.

The mule would find it hard to shake off any pursuers that might come their way.

Luckily for them, spare horses had to be kept for the coach in case any of them went lame or was used up. This meant that three animals were kept in the stables at the side of the ranch. Iron Hand looked at the three animals and discovered that one of them was a sorrel almost as big as the one ridden by his companion. He took to the animal at once. Luckily he also discovered a spare saddle in reasonable condition in the stables which he fitted on to the animal with the skills he had used in his old trade.

He did what he could for his mule, turning him out into the big field at the back of the Wright spread and making sure that he had water to drink and grass to eat. Bear was not too understanding of this care because to him an animal was just there to do what he wanted. He was not cruel to his horse, but if it died for any reason he would just get another and barely think about the old one.

'Come on,' he said, 'time to go.'

Iron Hand mounted his new steed, which he called Murphy after a gambler he had known. He looked back at the ranch.

'I hope he'll be all right,' he said, thinking of the animal that had saved his life. 'When all this is over, I'm coming back to get him.'

'Not all over yet,' said Bear, 'long way to go.' He cast an expert eye over the trail in front of him. 'They have many miles on us.' Then there was a commotion behind them; they could hear the sound of beating hoofs in the distance.

'You know that posse we mentioned earlier?' asked Iron Hand.

'Uh-huh white man.'

'I think they might have caught our scent.' As he said this Iron Hand spurred his new mount forwards, leaving his friend behind for a few seconds until the Indian caught up with him. Together, the sound of their would-be hunters behind them, they rode out of town for the duration.

The hunters had become the hunted.

CHAPTER FIFTEEN

Colonel Redmond sat in his office in Fort Morgan. He had a desk, but at the moment he was sitting in the red armchair to the left of the blue-painted door that led to his domain, smoking a cigar and contemplating the drawing on the wall opposite. It was a sketch of his wife and child as they had been all those years ago, etched on paper by one of the other officer's wives barely a month before they both died at the hands of the savages. His job had been partly to suppress the Indians so that the area could be exploited for the use of settlers and for the plentiful mineral resources that lay barely hidden in the hill country, but the death of his wife and child had meant that he pursued that aim with a little more zeal than necessary.

Not a day passed without thoughts of his loss bearing down on him. He had never remarried even though more than one female visitor had set her cap at him. He was a big, once-vigorous man who was now growing older and more thoughtful about some of the battles he had commenced and some of the things he had done.

It was not that he was growing 'soft' as far as he was concerned, but that he was starting to see the country grow in commerce and the need for military occupation in this area fade away quite rapidly now that most of the tribes had been subdued and relocated.

He would renounce his commission soon, go back home to Denver, where his family had grown rich from the gold gained in the Pike's Peak gold rush of the 1860s, and live out the rest of his life. Perhaps when he was away from the military world he would be able to forget, getting on with his life. Money would not be a problem, but it was amazing how money could never solve all of life's problems. He was just finishing his cigar when there was a knock on the door.

Reluctantly the Colonel heaved himself out of his armchair and stood ready for the intrusion. 'Come in,' he barked, and a young lieutenant entered, saluting as he did so. Johnson, his oldest serving aide was away on compassionate leave after the death of his oldest son. Colonel Redmond saluted back.

'Sir, there's a visitor who wants to see about an urgent matter,' said the young man.

'What kind of visitor? One of those do-gooders from the town?' growled the Colonel.

'No, it is a Mr Lemaitre, he says that you will want to see him.'

'Claude Lemaitre?' Colonel Redmond looked faintly astonished. He knew the hunter well for a very good reason. Trappers and hunters were used to travelling all over the state to ply their trade. They knew every nook and cranny of their own particular area and were

119

extremely useful in keeping track of the people in whom the army were interested. They were also excellent guides, cutting many days off any expeditions that had to be made into what might be unexplored territory for the military.

'I am not aware of any uprisings in the area,' said the Colonel. 'If he needs to sell anything, tell him to deal with the store men who deal with such things.' Again it was not unknown for those who cooked for the men to buy fresh meat off hunters, saving them from sourcing it from butchers in the town.

'He hasn't come about anything like that; except for a bag, he seems to be fairly empty-handed.'

'Then send him away, I don't need to have anything to do with him.'

'Very good sir.' The young man turned to go out of the still open door. 'I don't suppose you have any need of the message then?'

'I thought you had told me what he said.'

'I beg your pardon, he also said that he wanted you to know that he has information about someone called "Claire", and that you would know what he was talking about. Shall I still tell him to go sir?' Lieutenant Hart gazed at the Colonel who seemed to have been turned to stone. 'Are you all right, Colonel Redmond? Shall I just send him away?'

'Of course I'm all right,' barked the Colonel, 'now stop wasting time, man, and show him in.' The aide left knowing that his superior was not fine at all from the red flush on his features and the shallowness of his breathing. As soon as the young man had left, Redmond found his way to the seat behind his desk, moving almost blindly as if his eyes were focussed elsewhere.

Lemaitre entered the room looking remarkably dapper for a man who had just travelled many miles as the driver of a coach and-four. The fact was that it was early evening, and before coming here he had stopped off in town to make some living arrangements, taking the time to spruce himself up in the process.

'You wanted to see me?' The Colonel was now thin-lipped. 'What did you mean by using that name? Are you trying to provoke me in some way? Come on, out with it!' He rose from behind the desk in a threatening manner, but the Frenchman did not turn so much as a single hair. He put the flat, leather container he carried on to the Colonel's desk.

'It is good to see you again as well, my friend. When I complete what I have to say you will be offering me some of the best brandy from that cabinet over there.'

'That's as maybe. What are you here for?'

'I will take a seat and you will too then we will discuss the matter as two civilized men. That is the way to go about these matters.' Lemaitre sat opposite the Colonel in a plain wooden chair that was for those who needed to discuss matters with him across the oak desk. The man was an upstart who should have been ordered out of the building straight away, but for some reason his bearing demanded that he should be heard.

'You lost your wife and daughter a few years ago, is that not the case?'

'I thought you were here to discuss business! I do not want to talk about such matters.'

121

'Ah, but this is a form of business, to me at least. One which carries with it a trace of hope for you. But first we must discuss money.'

'What?'

'I have news that is worth a great deal of money. We all have to live, do we not? I want $50,000 from you and a signed assurance that the money is mine. You will give me the money in the form of a cheque. This cheque, it will be put in the bank in town to be cleared and only then will you be given access to your treasure.'

'I'll have nothing to do with you, or your stupidity,' said Colonel Redmond, beginning to stand up. 'This travesty of a meeting is over.'

'Then you will not want to see this.' The Frenchman's hand hovered over the leather document holder. Despite his feelings, the Colonel wanted to see what Lemaitre had with him. He sat down, a grim expression on his face as his visitor withdrew the pictures from within and put them in his hand. Redmond studied them in silence for a full minute.

'What trickery is this?'

'No trickery, Colonel. These are recently taken photographs of a young woman who, until recent times, has been living in a remote valley far from prying eyes. You see, she was to them as precious a gift as she is to you.' The Colonel laid down the photographs, looking suddenly old and tired beyond his years. 'I cannot bring your wife back, but your daughter I can.'

'Then for humanity's sake, do it now.'

'We are both businessmen Colonel. You give me my cheque and I will bring you Claire.'

'This is blackmail. I won't have it.'

'Very well, I shall leave and not return, thanking you for your time.'

'What's to stop me detaining you and getting the truth out of you by any means?'

'I have told my associates that if I do not return the girl is never to see you. We understand one another?' The blood drained from the face of the girl's father.

'Damn you, I'll do it. It's the simplest course of action, but if you harm her in any way. . . .' He angrily opened his desk and scribbled a cheque for the required amount. His family had made their fortune from gold and he had plenty of funds in reserve. He signed the contract as well that was proffered to him by his visitor before slumping back in his chair.

'Thank you.' Lemaitre gathered up his pieces of paper. 'I leave now. You are doing the right thing to help your daughter. When the cheque is cleared, within the day and the money is in my account I will have her brought to you.'

'Get out, you blackmailing piece of horseshit!' roared the Colonel, but Lemaitre needed no urging and was gone before he finished the sentence. The Colonel looked out of the window and watched as the dapper Frenchman made his way out of the fort. He was going to see his daughter again; she had survived. The money was nothing to him for that reason.

Well almost nothing. He called in his young lieutenant, Hart.

'Hart, I have just completed a rather delicate business transaction with that gentleman whom you just saw out

123

of the fort. Do me a favour, dress up as a civilian and keep an eye on him. You can stay in the town. Just report back where he goes and what he does.'

'Is this military business, sir?'

'Yes,' said the Colonel, lying for the sake of his money. 'Now don't stand about man, go, you have a lot of work to do.'

He stood at the window again. The twilight had deepened, throwing the buildings of the fort into deep shadow, his mind filled with thoughts of his daughter and wife and what he would do to Lemaitre if he was lying.

CHAPTER SIXTEEN

The posse was not too hard to shake off. This was because of the simple fact that, headed by the deputies who had discovered their sheriff tied up in a cell, there simply hadn't been enough time to organize a proper team. After finding out where the two men had gone from the owner of the livery where they had reclaimed their mounts, they had simply come across town to give chase. If the two had remained at the ranch there might have been a chance of catching them, but the horses used by the posse – which only consisted of four men anyway, the deputies and two citizens hastily roped in to help – were already tired and no match for those of the Indian and his companion who soon outpaced them once out in the wilds surrounding the town.

At one point the pursuers came close enough to the two men they were chasing to fire at them, but shooting from horseback was difficult and the bullets did not even come close. Then the riders lost sight of their prey completely in some particularly difficult terrain consisting of a gully with tall spires of rock, and gave up heart soon after.

Because the pair had not set out until well after midday it soon became clear that they were not going to catch up with their prey that same day, so once they considered themselves to be safe they took their time so that they did not wear out the horses. Finally, by mutual agreement, they found shelter in a low valley just outside Keensburg and settled down for the night. Due to their location they were even able to make a low fire out of brushwood and have some cooked meat and hot coffee.

Iron Hand had been looking thoughtful for some time. Now he looked at his companion, who sat cross-legged across from him in an impassive manner.

'He-Who-Hunts-Bear, I'm suffering from some serious doubts.'

'What do you mean?'

'Out of all the places we could go to, you decided that this oddball was going to go to Denver? Why not to another town or even out of the state altogether?'

'Maybe there are questions white man shouldn't ask; after all we know we're on their trail right now.'

'See, I got into this because Lemaitre robbed me of a great deal of money and I was angry enough to try and get some of it back. But now I'm beginning to think that you're not telling me the whole truth about what you know.'

'We are after joint enemy, is that not good enough for you, Iron Hand? What do you need to rake up past for? What is past is past.' The large man remained seemingly impassive as he said this, his voice calm and reasoned.

'So, answer my question, how did you know to track him down to Denver?'

'Sometimes truth not necessary, what happen now is good enough.'

'So, you need a little encouragement?' Iron Hand suddenly whipped out his Colt from an inside pocket. 'Gonna tell me what I want to know?'

'Put that away.' Slowly the big Indian moved his legs so that he was now on his haunches.

'Stop moving! You've been putting me in real danger and I want to know why. Tell me what I want to know, it ain't fair otherwise.' He waved the weapon. This was perhaps not the right thing to do due to the fact that Bear flushed red across his face and neck, as the anger at being threatened took him over so that he acted without any thought of consequences. He gave a roar that seemed to shake the very ground beneath their feet and sprang straight across their low campfire in his moccasins, completely ignoring any possible danger that might be inflicted by the flames and red-hot charcoal. As he sprang forwards Iron Hand, who had stood up when he drew his weapon, jumped backwards and away from the man who was now his opponent. He turned the weapon once more on the Indian, his good hand trembling as he did so, but with a look of utter contempt Bear slapped the weapon out of his hand. It went off with a loud bang, the bullet whining off harmlessly into the darkness as Bear picked up Iron Hand by the front of his jacket and flung him on to the ground.

Bear gave another wordless growl and reached down to pick up the former gambler, but as he did so Iron

127

Hand thumped him on the side of the head with his metal appendage. The Indian gave a grunt of pain and reeled backwards, staggering against the fire. From Iron Hand's angle he looked gigantic. The man lying on the ground also knew that the big Indian would not make the same mistake twice and that he was now going to die, as once more Bear lurched forward.

'Talk about regrettin' a question,' said Iron Hand, scrabbling to his feet. 'Just hit me with a rock and get it over with quick.' A look of surprise came across the Indian's face.

'I not going to kill you, Iron Hand, was going to pick you up and talk to you last time but you clonked me on side of head. Hurt like hell.' He shook the said object, looking mildly surprised. 'Was angry at your questions, but not now. Seems you have right to know when I think of it.'

'I still don't understand.' Iron Hand was still trembling in shock at the sudden attack that was over so soon. 'Guess I won't be asking you too many questions in future.'

The two men faced each other with the flickering campfire glowing in the space between them, half their faces in shadow.

'Like this,' said Bear, 'he tell me where he is going.'

'What? Lemaitre told you, when he was with the tribe, that he was going to take White Dove to Denver?'

'Not like you think. You see, he knew that I was special to White Dove, and he saw way of getting to her through me. I have always tried to go with the white man and his ways, even though he took so much away from

128

us. I learn some of his ways and help those like Lemaitre who help us.'

'And he took from that that you would help him trade in the girl?'

'He came across story about girl taken by Utes to be exchanged at later date, but who was now dead. He had been in the mountains before and found our tribe moved away from our hunting grounds. That was when he met White Dove for the first time.' Bear sighed as he thought about those times. 'Luckily for white man I was ill at time with fever or I would have killed some and not be here, despite learning about your ways and respecting them. You took much from us in a way that could not be forgiven. But during that time my tribe kept her face and body covered so no one suspect she was with us.'

'Why?'

'My father, Great Bear, he never have female child, only sons, he look on her as his daughter.'

'So what was your reaction to this offer?'

'I tell him to put it where sun don't shine, especially when he tell me that he has one who can say she is kidnapped girl.'

'Then why didn't you get him thrown out of your tribe or killed?'

'Because shortly after rumours about me start and then he is gone, with White Dove as his new woman. She told my father she wanted to go, and when he say no she did not fight him with words, but with actions.'

Iron Hand mulled this over.

'So what you are really saying is that he set you up

beforehand but that White Dove went willingly?'

'Yes.'

'Then why all this fighting? You could have avoided the whole thing.'

'No, you don't understand, he takes her back to her father. I lose her. That's why I did not tell you about hotel, and how Lemaitre knew man who died in number fourteen.'

'What about room fourteen?' There is an old saying that confession is good for the soul and it seemed that Bear was taking the opportunity to tell everything.

'Man who died there was brought up with White Dove, he would know her. Did not die in drunken fit at all.'

'You knew this.' Then a light went on in Iron Hand's head. 'You son of a bitch, you knew those men were going to come to the hotel and attack us. That's why you were up so early. You could've had me killed.' This time Iron Hand really did feel that he had been set up. He decided that this might be the time for them to part company. He would simply ride into town, get some kind of menial job and wait there until his former friend was gone. Bear would never risk the disapproval of the townsfolk by coming in and trying to capture a white man. Down that route lay the possibility of being shot or hanged.

'No, on my word, did not know about the men. They came to kill us for money they were promised. I was just up early, eager to get to White Dove.'

Bear, knowing what he did, must also have known that Lemaitre would try to protect his investment.

130

Having the money from the gold, he would find it not too difficult to recruit those in the local community who put themselves up for such tasks. Hired thugs would also know, from the investigations that the two had made, where they were staying. The key fact was whether Bear would risk such intrusions to get to his woman. If so, he might have thought they were going to be attacked at some point, but not in a specific place, which meant he too could not have predicted the arrival of the two men at the hotel. Iron Hand studied the Indian's face for what seemed like an eternity but in truth could only have been a few seconds.

'I'll believe you. I don't have much choice, Bear, but something tells me you've come out with the facts as you see 'em.'

'Good, then we sleep and look next day.' It was not the warmest night. They went to their respective tents and wrapped themselves up against the cold. Iron Hand lay awake for a long time; for the first time since he had started out, this trip had come to mean more than the money and he did not know what to do.

When daylight came neither of them discussed the matter much with each other. Both knew that time was an issue if they had to get to the girl so they rode onwards. At first they were both cold, but as the sun began to rise it put a little more warmth into their limbs – even so they did not break their silence but continued to allow their horses' hoofs to eat up the long miles. They had skirted the town of Keensburg by going along an arroyo. It was summer and smaller riverbeds often

131

dried up at this time of year, especially where the going was steep. It meant that they did not have to divert from their mission by too many miles.

The former gambler was in two minds about completing the trip because he knew that they could not end their time here without coming into some kind of conflict. When he thought they were going to be dealing with just Lemaitre he could never have predicted the crimes he would commit just to free his companion. Now it looked as if there might be more where that came from.

At last they rested so that they could have some of the beef jerky and beans they had brought with them while the horses rested for an hour, cropped the grass and drank from the nearest stream. Then they slept for another hour. It was a rest that they could ill afford because every minute they delayed meant that the girl was slipping from their hands. On the other hand, Iron Hand did not mind it at all because he was beginning to think he did not want to find out what had happened to her. He didn't know the woman, had no responsibility towards her. After all, he was just in this to try and recover some of the money that had been so ruthlessly taken from him.

'I have to ask you something,' said Iron Hand. 'What are you going to do with White Dove?'

'You do not want to know.' This was a statement that he had feared.

'You're going to kill her for breaking with your tribe, aren't you?'

Bear looked at him wordlessly for a few seconds as he

finished chewing on some of the tough jerky, then he burst out laughing. It was as if Iron Hand had unleashed a tide of humour in him. He laughed loud and long.

'You, white man, you think because she break tribe honour I have to hunt her down and take her life. What, with ritual? Tie her to totem and dance around her whooping?'

'Something like that.' Iron Hand found that he was feeling a little sheepish.

'I want her because she my betrothed and damn good-looking woman,' said Bear. 'Besides, Great Bear throw me out of tribe because of what he thinks I did, this is my way of telling him no.'

'So if we can get her, you will end this right now? No more killing if we can help it?'

'You're the one who want to kill Lemaitre.'

'I want some money out of him first, but if he's been splashing it around, hiring help and going this far to get what he wants, I doubt if there will be much left.'

'You don't know truth of it yet. Better to find out than never know.'

This was so obviously true that Iron Hand did not have an answer to what his possibly former friend had just said.

'Come on,' he said in the manner of one who has just been bettered and doesn't like to face the fact, 'pack everything up and let's get out of here.' By that time they had rested for a couple of hours, and although both of them were unhappy about the delay it was time they both needed. It was still many miles to the town of Fort Morgan and the sun was high in the sky. Even though they were not travelling in desert conditions it was still hot enough for them both to sweat as they continued, while the horses slowed down perceptibly as the long miles passed under their hoofs. Iron Hand began to lose any sense of hope that he might have had. They were on a trail that might end up colder than cold.

So much for vengeance.

CHAPTER SEVENTEEN

Matters were taking a strange turn at the old ranch that White Dove had been taken to. Jack had spent another night on guard, with the girl in one of the rooms, this time leaving her cuffed to an iron bed, the two manacles joined together with a longish chain so she had room to move without hurting herself. But at least she was now able to lie on a mattress. She had put in her protest after her arrival, when he asked her to settle down for the evening.

'What's your name, by the way? You never told me.'

'Jack.'

'Jack? What a good name. A simple name, yet one that seems to give you an air of a man people can trust. I like that name.' At this point she was sitting on the straw-filled mattress, one handcuff around her wrist and the other attached by the chain to a rather ornate curlicue in the iron frame. The place might be run down, but the owners had obviously been reasonably well-off from their cattle investments at one time because the place held a lot of good-quality furniture like the bed and even one or two paintings of country scenes on the walls.

'Just lie down real easy on that bed and get some sleep. The Frenchie seems to think this'll be over real soon.'

'Do I have to wear these clothes? I can't sleep properly with these on. I'm sure you know what I mean.' In actuality he was slightly baffled by her comments since he was quite used to sleeping in his clothes in the shack he shared with his two brothers, especially after they had been for a drunken night out. But he guessed women were different.

'Could you do me a favour and get me my real clothes?' She said this lightly as if asking for no particular favour. He remembered that his new boss had brought a trunk with him in the coach. He guessed that her former garments might be amongst them. The thing was, she was smiling at him as she asked for the favour and goldarnit if he could not find it in his soul to resist that smile. There was something in the way she looked at him seemed to bear a hint or a promise. He was not a wise man in the first place, but neither was he the first man to be moved to obey the words of a girl with a pretty smile. The trunk was still in the coach and he had to go outside to where they had concealed the vehicle between two outbuildings. He had brought an oil lamp with him and searched inside, bent over, with one hand, while holding the lamp with the other. He found her old clothes there, an Indian maiden costume made of soft buckskin with fringes in the middle and at the bottom of the skirt along with a belt to hold the skirt up. There was also a leather band to put around the top of her head to hold her hair in place and stop it from getting into her eyes.

He went back into the bedroom and deposited the clothes on the bed beside her, being careful to keep out of her reach.

'Silly man! How am I going to get changed with these cuffs on?' This was so obviously true that he did what she wanted and uncuffed her wrist from the chain, leaving the other cuff on the bed frame. 'You will at least turn your back or walk out?' she asked. Jack suddenly found that his mouth was very dry indeed. His heart was hammering and a pulse was beating on his forehead. He was barely twenty-two and had been brought up without much in the way of social graces, but he knew that what he was experiencing was nothing less than lust for the young woman sitting just yards from him who was about to get undressed.

'I'll leave you in peace,' he gasped before lurching from the room and closing the door with an unnecessary bang. He was not able to handle the way he felt about her, and knew that he had to get away from her as soon as he could or he might do something he would regret. He stamped about outside for a short while, but long enough for her to have changed back, and then he went to the door, shouting through,

'Are you ready ma'am?'

'Certainly.' He went in and she stood there looking every inch the Indian maiden. Where the more formal garments had somehow made her prim and proper despite her beautiful smile, she now looked so wild and free that he found his heart racing again and other parts further down reacting in a perfectly natural manner. He chained her up again quickly, gun in hand, fumbling with the key with the other.

There was a bed in one of the rooms beside hers. He lay down on this aware that his heart was hammering. He could think of nothing but the young woman next door. He did not have to wait long before he heard her voice through the thin wooden wall that divided the two rooms.

'Jack, where are you? Could you come and see me?'

Her tone was far from being one of anger and it brought him to his feet in seconds. He went into her room. This could not be happening, he said inside his head, he had his duty to his brothers and he couldn't let some woman get in the way of their ranch. They were dealing with trouble back there in Denver, he would have to do the same here. As he walked into the room she was on the bed straining at the bonds that held her there. Once more he cursed her for having such a beautiful face and figure.

'Jack, let me out of these chains for just a little while. They're hurting me. I'm sure that guy wouldn't mind if you did so. He's obviously in business, and I'm his to trade. He wouldn't like it if I was damaged in any way.'

'You're trying to trick me.'

'What if I am? You're the clever one; you've got the gun and the upper hand.' The way she was lying down, raising her head to speak to him, did something to him that he could not describe. Of course he was the one in charge, there was no doubt about that and he had permission to subdue her if she tried anything on. Besides, he was at least six inches taller and weighed about sixty pounds more. She wouldn't be any match for him.

Having wrestled with his inner doubts then putting them firmly to rest, he went over and unlocked her restraints once more, stepping back as soon as she was free with his gun pointed at her to prevent any strange goings-on from occurring.

'I'll give you half an hour to free yourself up, then you're getting chained again. Best thing for you.'

She rubbed her wrists and stood up, but slowly so that she did not antagonize him in any way. She paced up and down the room for a short while. What disconcerted him most was that she asked him questions while she did so about his brothers, his mother and father and where his family came from originally. However although his gun was not lowered, this talk did serve to bring down his guard and make him more relaxed, which had been exactly her attention. Now she stood beside the bed and faced him full on.

'Jack, I saw the way you were looking at me earlier.'

'We don't need to talk about that, ma'am.'

'Do you know that you're a fine looking boy? Just a couple of years older than me, and that's exactly right. Do you know that He-Who-Kills-Bear is at least ten years older than his girl? Bit of an age gap.'

'Wait a minute,' Jack fastened upon the name, 'who is he?'

'The man I was supposed to marry in our tribal ceremony in front of the medicine man with our totem to
the gods behind him, he's the man who will be looking
for me right now. But he isn't important.'

'What?'

'You are. Look at me Jack, what do you think?' She
was wearing a fringed blouse, which was held together at
the front by a hide drawstring. As she spoke she pulled
on this and the front of the garment drew back reveal-
ing a pair of beautiful breasts the like of which he had
never seen in his life before, given that he was used to
dealing with whores with somewhat raddled bodies.
This was a young woman with a body that had been nur-
tured on good, natural foods and was largely untouched
by the trials of life.

'I don't really need an answer,' she said demurely,
'given that you're pointing something else at me beside
that silly gun of yours.' She sat on the edge of the bed
and spread her legs open. She had long, shapely limbs
of a brown colour that came straight from Mother
Nature and he felt drawn to her as if he was made of
metal and she was a magnet. As he approached her he
holstered his gun, more concerned with the anticipa-
tion of what was to come. She laughed as she drew him
down to nuzzle his shaggy head between her breasts. He
was in pure heaven as he was filled with the the scent of
her glowing skin, which was the point where she drew
the gun out of holster and whacked him as hard as she
could on the back of the head. He gave an injured grunt
and slid to the floor between her legs.

Knowing that she did not have much time she undid

the chains from the bed and locked his wrists together where he lay, her pink-tipped breasts swinging as she did so. After completing her task she laced her garment back up, and as she did so looked down upon his supine form.

'It's a pity, you really are a good-looking boy. Mind you, you smell like a pig who's just rolled in his own filth.' On the way out of the room she made sure that the door was locked in case he managed somehow to get to his feet, kick it open and come out after her. Even with his hands bound he might turn out to be dangerous after the way she had destroyed his male pride.

As she left the room it was early evening and not yet dark, just as she had anticipated. She had not wanted to seduce him, but once she was dressed like her old self, her thoughts had led her to the consideration that it was all she could do.

She began to go out of the building to get one of the horses grazing in the nearby field when she heard the rattling of chains.

'You bitch, what've you done to me? I'll kill you!' She gave a smile of satisfaction as she closed the door behind her and stepped out on to the porch. As she did so a shadowy figure jumped on her from behind, wrapped strong arms around her and lifted her off her feet. So tight was he holding her that she was even unable to scream.

For all her efforts, she had been recaptured.

141

CHAPTER EIGHTEEN

White Dove started to kick against her captor and found that she was looking at the muzzle of a gun held by a wiry-looking man. He stared at her for a second or two then dropped his arm and holstered the weapon.

'Sorry ma'am, we thought you was one of the enemy, it being shadowed here like.' The figure that was holding her put her down and she whirled around to find she was facing the stern figure of Bear. His strong features seemed to melt momentarily then he held her at arm's length. It was not the custom of his tribe to show much in the way of affection. The girl stared at him.

'You! But I thought you were miles behind them.'

'We were. Now we are here, you come with us. We take you back.'

'I'm not going back.'

'No use to say that, you come with us.'

'Listen to me. The reason I left with Lemaitre was because I wasn't happy. You know why.' Her former would-be mate shuffled a little at this. If it hadn't been for the fact he was a fierce-looking warrior, Iron Hand would have said that Bear was embarrassed.

'Bear, what's she talking about?'

'He didn't tell you, did he? I suppose he roped you into coming after me with some story that I went away against my will, a poor kidnapped girl.'

'Something like that, ma'am.'

'Well the truth is a lot more complex. I grew up with the tribe, Great Bear's adopted daughter, but I was able to see even from the early days that I wasn't one of them. I fell for this one here when I was ten years old and he was already a big man of eighteen.'

'He does not need to know,' said Bear. 'You come with us right now.'

'No, I won't until I've told someone the truth. I was happy to be with the tribe. They were my family now and they did not mean me any harm, in fact the opposite. But I knew from speaking to missionaries who came to stay with us from time to time that I was different, even though at first I could not remember my life before coming to them. But look at the way I speak my own tongue so fluently – missionaries again.'

'You were special one for our tribe, good luck for us,' said Bear.

'I thought that was a true story. I liked the life in the mountains. Then the tribe were moved to that desolate valley. I hated it there and I wanted to go back to the place I loved the most. Some good luck charm I was by then.'

'Wait, I can guess the rest,' said Iron Hand, 'you asked this big guy to help you return. All you needed

143

was each other and you could live a life of peace even if you had to leave the tribe. It broke your heart to do it, but you just weren't going to spend the rest of your life in some godforsaken place.'

'I guess you're a mind-reader, mister.'

'My name is Iron Hand. I used to have another title, but that's what I call myself now.'

'Then the trapper came along. . . .'

'We can guess what happened. It broke your heart to leave this guy but it was the same story. Lemaitre promised you a brighter future. You're young, you believed him.' The girl bent her head, and for the first time in a while tears started to fall.

'We go, take you back where you belong.' She raised her head and gazed fiercely at her betrothed.

'You don't understand, I want to stay here and wait for the return of Lemaitre. And for other reasons too.'

'But why wouldn't you take the chance to leave?' asked Iron Hand.

'Mister, there must be a reason why you teamed up with Bear.'

'There was.'

'Was your reason connected with this Lemaitre?'

'I guess you could say so.' He glanced down at his artificial appendage, the look telling her the entire story.

'Well I want to see the end of this business as much as you do. I want to see Claude Lemaitre pay for his actions.'

'I want this too,' said Bear simply. He looked at Iron Hand.

'You too?'

'What do you think?'

*

On the previous day Lemaitre left Fort Morgan and went into town where he went to the Bank of Colorado and deposited the cheque along with the signed contract from Colonel Redmond. Unfortunately for him he had to wait at least a day while the bank wired through to Denver to make sure the funds were available from Redmond's account. He was not a great drinker but he went to the nearest hotel and celebrated his triumph on his own with a good brandy and retired to bed. Lieutenant Hart reported all this to the Colonel the same night.

'It looks like he won't be going anywhere until at least the morning,' said Hart.

'Then we will get ready for when he does.' The next day the Colonel prepared his sword and a military pistol and dressed in a grey cloak since the day was cold. He had prepared four soldiers to accompany him and five horses; those men were also armed. This was a total breach of military protocol, since he was employing army resources to his own ends. It was an offence for which he could be court-martialled if it ever came to light. On the other hand, he was trying to help recover his daughter so it was understandable that he would try and use any means at his disposal even if this did break with acceptable military protocol. There was another, underlying reason for his behaviour and it was simply that being with the army had caused the death of his wife and the loss of his child, so they could damn well help him out at a time of need.

145

As with all situations within the army, this operation was carried out on a need-to-know basis.

'There's a problem with the natives,' he told them, 'possible Apache involvement, and I want us to be on the lookout for intrusions within the area. You are under my direct orders, so don't take any action without my personal commands.'

Hart soon arrived and told the Colonel that his target had moved out. Not wanting to scare him off in any way, the Colonel waited for a short while.

He could have captured Lemaitre easily, but he had taken the man at his word that no amount of torture would make him reveal where the girl was. Besides – and his blood ran cold at the thought – if he resorted to such illegal methods with someone who was a private citizen, criminal or not, the word would soon get about and he would be relieved of his command and disgraced in the process. He also believed that Lemaitre would have made sure that the girl was killed if he did not return at a set time.

His troops, including Hart, looked at each other a little warily as they moved out. Many of them had thought he was a little strange, for the loss of his wife and child had hit him badly over the years but they did not know what to make of this latest behaviour. There had been no uprisings or any trace of them around here for a long time. But they followed in his wake as he rode out of town, doing what all soldiers did and blindly following their leader.

CHAPTER NINETEEN

Lemaitre took the fork in the road that led to the old ranch. He was lucky in that he knew the local geography well, and the stories of those who lived in the area. The ranch had been owned by a cattleman called Goodman. Unfortunately, with the end of the Indian wars the need to supply a large garrison at the fort had dried up and Goodman had been forced to sell up and retire to the East along with his family. If he had been able to get some of the lucrative contracts to supply beef to the tribes who were sequestered on to reservations he might have done all right, but that business had gone to large consortiums who were able to give a kick-back to politicians in Washington, leaving the small trader unable to compete.

The ranch had been sold to a trader in Denver who had wanted to make something of it, but had never got round to doing so, preoccupied as he was with his business in that city. Lemaitre had known that trader and the ranch because he was a man who made connections in many places. That was why he was able to use it for his business. Whether or not the trader would have given him the keys to the place if he had known what that business was would have been another matter.

Lemaitre rode briskly towards the ranch; the route he took was heavily wooded on either side, with a flowing river to the left that could occasionally be seen through a gap in the trees. It was a cold day with the sun just rising over the horizon. He was going to release the girl just as he had promised, taking her to the outskirts of town and getting his employee to hold her there until he, Lemaitre took out the money and departed. That part of the deal at least would be straightforward enough. Once Jack took her to the fort that would be the end of the matter. They might arrest the young man, but that was not Lemaitre's concern, for he would be long gone by then.

He was not a man who trusted his colleagues, preferring to rely on his own judgement, so he did not approach the buildings directly. He wanted to see how Stapely was doing with his captive. This was another reason why he had left him alone with her for as little time as possible. She was a beautiful woman and he did not trust young cowboys with pretty women.

Having hitched his horse nearby, Lemaitre stole to the side of the building. He was rewarded by the sound of low voices out the front. One of them was that of the girl. He recognized the others too, and his blood began to boil. Why couldn't they just leave him alone? He was heavily armed, with a Colt 0.44 in a holster on either hip, having donned his gun belt before leaving the hotel. (He had considered it politic not to wear such a display at the fort the day before for the simple reason that it sent out a message that might have led to him not getting out of there.)

Lemaitre forced himself to calm down. He knew that three against one was not a good way to go, especially since they were going to be on the lookout for him.

And where was Jack?

He considered the matter for a minute then looked in the windows of the various rooms at the side and back of the building. It was through one of these that he saw the young man propped against the side of the bed, a mark on his forehead, looking distinctly sorry for himself. Lemaitre slipped through the open window and saw that the man sitting with his back to the bed was about to speak. His would-be rescuer shook his head and put a hand over his mouth to indicate silence. Jack understood and nodded. He would agree to anything to get free of his bonds.

Luckily Lemaitre was a thorough kind of person; although he had given Jack one set of keys for the various locks around the place he had kept the other set in a tightly buttoned pocket at the side of his cloth jacket. He took this out and found the right one with some difficulty because the room was in semi-darkness, inserted this into the lock and freed his employee, who stood up, rubbing his wrists. His rescuer, knowing the value of time, indicated that Jack should follow him outside. Soon they were at the side of the building. Lemaitre risked speaking to his employee in a whisper that hardly seemed louder than the rustling of the trees.

'You take this weapon please and go round the other

side. They were at the front a little while ago, we will ambush them.' Jack looked a little bemused at this.

'Say, why don't we just get outta here?'

'Two reasons. I want you to disarm the men so that we can capture them without the girl.'

'I'll blow their goldurn heads off so I will.'

'No you won't. Listen to me, we are practically finished here. We must make sure that they are captured, along with the girl. We will imprison them and then you will take the girl to the gates of Fort Morgan and leave her. If we kill the men she will tell all and we will be wanted refugees who will hang for murder. Savvy?'

Jack looked quite bitter at this. He had been tricked by a mere girl and now he was denied revenge on her and the two men with her.

'It ain't fair,' he protested.

'Life is not fair my friend,' said Lemaitre, continuing to whisper. 'How will your brothers feel if they find out that you have spoiled their chances of ever getting that place of their own? Have you considered that fact?'

He was shrewd enough to have said the one thing that would have persuaded the cowboy not to take his revenge. Jack did not like the thought of having to face his brothers and tell them that not only had he lost their money, but he was also a wanted man. They would refuse to have anything to do with him and he would end up in jail – or be hanged. He was not to know that far from getting their ranch, the only wooden structure they would now inhabit was a large box each.

'All right, I won't kill 'em,' he said.

'That is fine. Now go to the other side and wait. Try

150

not to let them hear you. When I have given you time, I will go to the front and hold them up, and when I shout your name you will come out and get them from another angle. Go now.'

Lemaitre waited for a few minutes. The building was not large and when he was sure that his companion was in place he began to move towards the front where his former pursuers were in deep conversation with the girl. It had only taken him a few minutes to free the young man and explain the situation to him, but in his mind it had taken hours. He felt a sheen of sweat on his fore-head as he stepped rapidly out to the front of the building.

'Put your hands up,' he said and just as he was preparing to shout to his companion, he found that he had a carbine pointed straight at his stomach by the man that he thought he had killed a long time ago.

The three people who had plagued him so much were standing as if they were posing for some kind of wide-set photograph. White Dove was in the middle with an inscrutable look on her pretty features, looking straight forward. Bear was to her right, looking to the far side of the building, war club in hand, although he turned as Lemaitre appeared, and Iron Hand was looking poised, finger on the trigger of his weapon.

'Well well, my old friend Claude,' said Iron Hand. 'I was expecting a more frontal approach, but I should have known what you would try. You're a devious bastard at the best of times, now put down your weapon or I'll drop you where you stand. You know, I had it in

151

mind that I would do precisely that when I found you, but I guess you're going back with me to find some kinda justice in Denver.'

'Jack wouldn't like this,' said Lemaitre in a loud voice and at that second a gravelled voice, affected by the lack of water, came from behind.

'Drop your weapons.' The other two turned to see that Jack was standing there, gun covering both Bear and his friend because he was far enough away to do so. If Iron Hand made the slightest attempt to pull the trigger the cowboy would be able to drop him in a second. Although he was well aware of this, Iron Hand did not drop his carbine because he knew that the Frenchman still held a Colt loosely at his side and that releasing his grip would be tantamount to signing his own death warrant.

He did not know that their enemy had pledged to keep them alive for 50,000 reasons that would remain in the bank until the cheque had been cleared, and even if he had done so he would still not have trusted the man whom he regarded as the human version of a black viper. Then Bear gave a roar that seemed to come from the very soles of his feet and all hell broke loose.

The Indian was still holding his axe with the blunt end facing towards the man who had just threatened them. He gave a seemingly innocuous flick of the wrist and then his war club flew straight at Jack. The weapon caught the cowboy in the chest and he made a noise like a cushion that had just had all the air expelled from it. The unexpected assault had the effect of making him unable to focus on his task – holding up the two men so that the girl could be isolated from them. He shot off two bullets at random, one of which whistled past Lemaitre's head, which had it gone home would have ended the events of the day there and then.

The other shot was discharged into the air as Bear jumped forward with a speed and alacrity that belied his size, grabbing the arm of the man who had aroused his great fury. Jack dropped the weapon because his arm was suddenly and painfully jerked upwards so that it felt to him as if it was being pulled from its socket. He was a tall man, though, about the same height as his attacker although not as well built, and he managed to pull away from Bear through sheer force and the desire to retain his right arm. Bear did not take kindly to this. He was filled with the kind of anger where he wanted to bring down his enemy and lay him out for good.

The two men had encountered each other so furiously that their impetus had carried them to a point beyond where their weapons lay, leaving them without the ability to pick either up. This meant that they were now meeting each other with naked fists. With a roar from Bear and a shout from Jack they set to it with a will.

While this was happening between the two fighters, another equally dramatic scene was unfolding on the other side of the building. Iron Hand, on hearing the gunshots, had swung his carbine round to defend his friend. It was a split second decision that could have cost him his life simply because Lemaitre too was armed, and for all he knew ready to kill those who remained.

Lemaitre was not slow to spot his opportunity and did

what he needed in order to secure the capture of the girl. The fistfight between the other two men was a mere detail that could be worked out later. He sprang forward with great agility and wrested the carbine away from his enemy, aided by the fact that he, Iron Hand, did not have the full use of two hands to grip more tightly. As the gun clattered to the ground Iron Hand turned to find the Colt pointed at his face.

It was in that split second that Lemaitre had to decide whether to kill his opponent in order to stop him from interfering with what he planned to do, or to let him live. The truth was, he had a third alternative that came midway between the two, and it was this course of action that the Frenchman decided to take. Coldly he aimed his gun at Iron Hand's legs as he prepared to shoot him in one of his knees. This kind of shot was quite common in these parts if you wanted to take out an opponent without killing him. The person shot in that manner would suffer so much personal agony they would lose interest in other matters for a very long time indeed, added to which they would be unable to get to their feet.

In his intent, Lemaitre had completely forgotten about the girl. White Dove crossed the space between the two men with such speed she could hardly be seen, giving a blood-curdling yell at the same time that showed she had learned well from her adopted tribe. She grabbed Lemaitre by the neck and began to strangle him with her young, sinewy hands. It would not be the first time in her young life she had carried out such an act.

To save his life at once, Lemaitre would have had to shoot her, which he was quite prepared to do, even though it would have meant the end of his plans, but at least he would still be alive to make his escape. Iron Hand saw what was about to happen and clubbed the man on the wrist with his metal hand, causing him to drop the weapon when his fingers became numb from the shock.

With a force that could only be described as relentless the girl bore down on her enemy, choking his life away, until Iron Hand grabbed her from behind and squeezed the bicep of her right arm so hard that it broke her grip lower down. Once this was done he began to pull her away from the man who was by now heading towards the ground as his legs buckled from under him.

'Not this way,' yelled Iron Hand into her ear. 'We need him – for Denver. He's the only proof we didn't kill those two fellas.'

'What fellas are you talking about?' she grated, rounding on him.

'Those brothers he hired to kill us.'

She did not really know what he was talking about but responded to the urgency in his voice and let go of the killer completely. Lemaitre lay there on the ground writhing about like a newly landed fish as he fought to fill his lungs, still clutching at his throat, his face an interesting shade of purple. Iron Hand pulled the girl further back as his eyes searched avidly for his weapon which was close to the fallen man. As he looked, he was dimly aware that he could hear the sound of horses' hoofs pounding towards them.

Jack, who was still slugging it out with Bear a few yards away, was well aware of what had been said. He pulled away from the big Indian with a hoarse shout and a look of horror that had nothing to do with their fight.

'What did he say about my brothers?' His heartfelt question had its own reply in what had already been said and it was not long before he too was nearly upon the recumbent man, fury having given him the strength of three men to break away from Bear. It was clear that he had a personal anger that would make him take drastic action against Lemaitre.

Even as the young man began to jump upon him, Lemaitre rolled over on to his back, seizing the carbine that lay nearby with both hands. Without thinking too much he levelled it at Jack and fired before the weapon was clubbed out of his grip and sent spinning away by Iron Hand, who was stricken by fury in seeing it in his enemy's possession. The move was far too late to save the would-be attacker because the shot hit Jack in the top of the leg, spinning him to the ground and laying him out so that he remained there, groaning, with blood coming from the wound. But the bullet had caught him in a fleshy part of the leg and he would live.

At this, the girl would have attacked Lemaitre again, but she did not have the chance.

'Halt, all of you, or you'll all be dead,' said an imperious voice. It was as if time froze. Lemaitre was penned in on one side by Bear and on the other by Iron Hand. The girl was in front of the fallen man. So intense was their attention on what they were doing that they had failed to see the cavalry officer advance. Now he stood there with his sword in one hand and a military Colt in the other. His gun was levelled at Bear and it was obvious that he was going to shoot him.

'You savages are nothing but trouble, helping this villain.' He was referring to the prone Frenchman. The girl flung herself in front of the man who had sought to find her. 'Your squaw won't save you.' Colonel Redmond's finger tightened on the trigger and then he looked into the face of the girl and his hand seemed to lose all its nerves as he let the weapon drop to the ground.

'Claire,' he said.

'Father!' replied the girl.

CHAPTER TWENTY

Business had been more or less taken care of when two men left Fort Morgan the next day. One was a big Indian who would once have been executed just for being near a place like this on the assumption that he had come here with murderous intent. The other was a wiry man with deep-set eyes who had suffered a lot of pain and loss in his time but now had a reward that would more than cover the money he had lost from his mining days, although the money would never be enough to compensate him for the loss of his hand. As the two men rode out on their respective mounts they both looked back and saw the girl once called White Dove standing at the gates of the fort with her father. She wore a dress much like the one foisted on her by Lemaitre during the bad times.

She waved at them for a moment, then turned and fled into the interior of the building, hand over her face. Her father followed at a more dignified pace with a nod to those who had helped him restore what was left of his family.

Bear watched them go with no expression on his strong features.

The two men rode on for a while in silence.

'I guess she couldn't have loved you as much as you thought,' said Iron hand at last.

'She does,' said Bear shortly.

'But why would you let her go? If I loved a woman I'd sure—'

'She had dream, many times, that told her to leave tribe and find family. That is why she went with killer, thinking he would help her, but he just using her for much of your money.' The Indian shook his head. 'This world belong to everyone but you make paper and suddenly paper means more than real things.'

'I still don't understand why you didn't fight to keep her.'

'She give me many presents, weavings and carvings in my tepee. I keep them to remind me of her. All those years she never forget in her deep mind where she come from. She must be with her father.'

Then Iron Hand understood the sacrifice behind what Bear had done, that the young woman who was supposed to be his would always be with him in his heart no matter what, and spoke no more on that subject.

'Great news, ain't it, that the old Colonel got behind us and believed our story about Denver now that he's got that rat Lemaitre in the hoosegow?'

'What he did?'

'Well the rat squealed just about all he could about sending those boys to kill us and how they was all scum, including the third one he wounded in front of the

Colonel and his men. By the way, that boy'll testify for us too. You watch, Colonel Redmond might be many things but he's a man of his word, he'll square it with Hinkman by wiring that lieutenant of his who's still out there, get it done in person. We have his word; he belongs to the old school. He'll see us right.' Bear gave a satisfied nod.

'What do you do now?'

'I guess I can go to Denver, buy a place and settle down, find a little wife,' said Iron Hand, looking straight ahead.

'Then I return to the mountains.'

'I guess so.' Iron Hand detected the underlying tone. 'You'll do well on your own, you can hunt, fish, live.'

'That is so, white man.'

'Who am I fooling? What the hell, I'm going with you, we're going back to your tribe and I'm going to tell them what happened. They might trust a man as beat up as I am. Claire – White Dove – is where she belongs. I can get them to accept that.'

'You do that for me?' Bear showed little emotion as was his way, but there was no mistaking the tone in his voice.

'Yes,' said Iron Hand, 'but first we got to go back to Denver.'

'Why?'

'For Mokie of course, he's not just a mule, he's a friend and not as stubborn as some humans, I can tell you.' He gave Bear a sly sideways glance and for the first time in a while his companion smiled.

The two of them rode onwards.

160